The truck's motor revved as it loomed behind Maya.

Should she call for help? She reached for her phone in the holder on her dash, but a sudden jerk had her bracing.

The truck had hit her bumper. And he was coming back for more.

Maya sped up, but she was no match for the attacker. He rammed her again, and she held tight to the steering wheel as her car veered off the shoulder. She corrected and pulled her SUV into the lane again.

Up ahead, the bridge over Coley Lake came into view. *Oh, no.* If he hit her again, she could go over the side. She pressed her gas pedal down as far as it would go, but the truck kept coming.

Another hit, then a loud pop. Her car swerved wildly to the right.

Her tire had blown! Maya struggled to control the vehicle, but it went into a spin. Her hands slipped from the wheel as the SUV hit the guardrail...and plunged over the side.

Hope Welborn is an award-winning author of spine-tingling suspense, sprinkled with romance and saturated with faith. By day, she masquerades as a digital content marketing technologist, and by night, she stays up too late putting words on the page. When not writing, she loves to spend time on her family's farm in the beautiful north Georgia mountains and play piano for her church.

Books by Hope Welborn

Love Inspired Suspense

Taken Without a Trace

Visit the Author Profile page at LoveInspired.com.

TAKEN WITHOUT A TRACE

HOPE WELBORN

LOVE INSPIRED SUSPENSE
INSPIRATIONAL ROMANCE

MIX
Paper | Supporting responsible forestry
FSC® C021394
www.fsc.org

LOVE INSPIRED® SUSPENSE
INSPIRATIONAL ROMANCE

PLEASE RECYCLE
THIS PRODUCT IS RECYCLABLE
Recycling programs for this product may not exist in your area.

ISBN-13: 978-1-335-91915-1

Taken Without a Trace

Love Inspired
22 Adelaide St. West, 41st Floor
Toronto, Ontario M5H 4E3, Canada
www.LoveInspired.com

HarperCollins Publishers
Macken House, 39/40 Mayor Street Upper,
Dublin 1, D01 C9W8, Ireland
www.HarperCollins.com

Printed in Lithuania

1 2 3 4 5 6 7 8 9 10 LIT 28 27 26 25

But now thus saith the Lord that created thee,
O Jacob, and he that formed thee, O Israel,
Fear not: for I have redeemed thee,
I have called thee by thy name; thou art mine.
—*Isaiah* 43:1

For A and J—never give up on the dreams
God has placed in your hearts.

And for my Suspense Squad sisters (Dana, Darlene,
Loretta, Patty, Sami, Shannon & Virginia)—
I wouldn't be here without you.

ONE

He was going to die. Special Agent Cash Brenner raced through the darkened warehouse, the Doberman pinscher on his heels. The dog's jaws snapped too close to Cash's ankle. Fear urged his legs to pump even harder. He'd never been mauled by a dog, and he didn't intend to find out what it would be like now. In his time with the Georgia Bureau of Investigation, he had been in tight spots before, but not like this.

"Cash? Cash!" The voice of Special Agent Owen Donnelly came through his earpiece. "What's happening?"

"Hang…on…" He skidded around a corner, trying to put distance between him and the Doberman.

The gun in his ankle holster did him no good as he couldn't stop long enough to retrieve it. Not that he would want to shoot an animal. But maybe he could at least scare it off.

"Where are you?" Owen asked.

"Pendleton," Cash managed between breaths.

"You're cutting out. Sounded like you said Pendleton."

"I did."

"What are you doing out there?"

Cash gritted his teeth. He knew better than to go in without his partner. But when the anonymous tip had come in with information on one of his missing person cold cases, he'd jumped in his car and headed for the location the caller had given.

No point alerting his team at the GBI's Appalachian Investigations Division until he was sure the tip was credible. They'd had too many false starts on the Fielding case to get anyone's hopes up now. The raspy voice on the line had told him to check out an old warehouse in the industrial park of Pendleton, a neighboring town to Gadden Valley, where Cash lived.

"I found something," he said. Something he couldn't tell his partner over the phone.

"What? I can't hear—" Static cut through the line.

Teeth snapped at his heels. He spied an old crate and threw it, but the dog dodged the projectile and came at him even faster.

"Say again?" Owen said. "Give me your location."

"I'm in a ware—"

A loud pop sounded behind him. Cash stumbled to his knees as a bullet whizzed by and lodged into the wall in front of him.

"Was that a gunshot?" Owen's voice reached a new octave.

Someone was here. And shooting at him. Game changer. Cash grabbed an old board and swung it at the Doberman. The dog ducked out of the way but paused long enough for Cash to scramble to his feet and take off again.

Had he been set up? Or just gotten too close to the truth about the cold case? Four years after Elizabeth Fielding had vanished, her disappearance remained unsolved. And it haunted him. Every agent had that one case that got under their skin. This was his. He worked the case in his off-hours every chance he got. But he'd never had a lead pan out. Not like it had tonight. And now someone wanted to make it very clear he shouldn't be here.

Another shot rang out.

"Cash, if you don't tell me right now—"

He had to find a way out of this building.

"Industrial park," he said.

"You broke up. Repeat?"

Where were the stairs to the first floor? He had to be coming to the end of the structure. And if he was, then he'd be trapped.

He headed toward a dim light up ahead. A large window let in the faint glow from the streetlight outside.

The snarl at his back alerted him to the dog's presence. The shock from the thrown board had only bought Cash a few moments, and now his pursuer was back with a vengeance.

No time to look for another outlet.

God, help me!

Cash aimed for the window and jumped.

A million stings slashed across his body as the glass shattered around him. He fell through the air, arms and legs flailing for something to grab. The loading dock below rushed up at him, and Cash landed. Hard. Pain shot through his left shoulder.

Over the ringing in his ears, he heard barking. The dog loomed in the window two stories above. At least the animal had more sense than to jump as Cash had.

A dark figure appeared beside the dog. Light glinted from the raised gun.

Cash rolled sideways off the dock, ducking as more shots came at him. He ran for the shadows surrounding the building.

"Owen?" No response. The earpiece was gone. Must've lost it in the fall. His brain felt like a Ping-Pong ball bouncing around in his head. Stars danced in his vision. His left arm throbbed, and he couldn't lift it. Probably dislocated it when he landed.

How long before the dog and its handler made it outside? This wasn't a time to go on defense. He was injured and fading fast. Unconsciousness threatened to pull him under, but he fought it, making it to his car. He probably shouldn't be driving but he had no other choice.

Another bullet ate up the gravel in front of him. He jumped into the car and peeled out of the parking lot, steering with his good hand.

A spot of light appeared behind him. Was his attacker giving chase? The industrial park was a maze of roads intersecting each other. If he could reach the main highway, he'd be home free.

The stabbing pain in his head was getting worse, and the road began to blur ahead of him. *Stay with it, Brenner.* He willed his eyes to focus, but it was a losing battle. The oblivion pulled harder.

Headlights bloomed in front of him. A horn blared. Cash wrenched the steering wheel, trying to maintain hold as the car spun out of control. Metal crunched as the car jerked to a hard stop.

Pain surrounded him as darkness closed in.

Private investigator Maya Reid's SUV skidded to the side of the road. She gripped the steering wheel as her heart beat wildly. *What just happened?*

Following a lead on her current case had brought her to the industrial park. At this time of night, she had expected to be alone. She hadn't seen anyone else in the area. Until now.

The car seemed to have come out of nowhere. Flying out of a side road of the industrial park, it had almost clipped her front fender. Then, it had careened off the road and slammed into a tree.

She grabbed her phone to call 911 but paused when a man emerged from the car. Opening her own door, she stepped out.

"Sir? Are you okay?"

He didn't seem to hear her as he stumbled, one hand held to his head. The other arm hung at an odd angle. Possibly broken or dislocated.

"Hey!" She spoke louder. "Sir? Can I help—"

The words died in her throat as he turned. *Cash Brenner?*

She hadn't seen him in over two years. Not since he'd carelessly ended things between them. And broken her heart.

Pushing the thought aside, she stepped toward him. "Cash?"

Crystal-blue eyes met hers, and her breath caught. She'd forgotten how piercing his gaze could be.

But his eyes looked through her, not seeming to recognize her. "Go." He glanced at the road behind them. "Have to…go."

"You're not going anywhere." A deep cut at his temple mingled with his short, dark hair. He probably had a concussion. "You need medical attention."

He took two steps and almost toppled. Definitely a concussion.

She positioned herself next to his good shoulder and braced under the impact of his weight. Maya was not a tiny woman, but Cash was a big man. Tall and muscular.

She directed him away from the wreck. "Let's get you to my car, and I'll call for help."

He mumbled something that sounded like—

"Bones? Yeah, you probably have something broken. We'll let the paramedics che—"

The sound of another motor caught her attention. A sleek, dark street bike skidded to a halt at the edge of the pavement. Before she could speak, the rider raised a weapon.

Shoving Cash ahead of her, Maya ducked behind his car as a spray of bullets flew at them. Metal pinged as the shots bit into Cash's Mustang. The gunman meant business.

And she was unarmed. Her SIG P365 was tucked next to the seat in her SUV. Too far away to reach before a bullet found her.

She was usually more careful when working a case. This one had her head spinning. Her sister was missing.

Now she was being shot at. And with her ex-boyfriend, of all people.

Cash moaned on the ground. Had he been hit? She scanned him. No gunshot wounds. He struggled to reach toward his foot. An ankle holster peeked at the edge of his pants leg.

He was in no condition to fire a weapon.

"I got it." She grabbed the gun. A Glock 22. Not her preferred choice, but it would do. There was probably some law against using a GBI agent's firearm, but desperate times and all…

She racked the slide, hoping the magazine was full.

Crawling to the rear bumper, she checked the shooter's location. She'd never fired a weapon at an actual human, but she wasn't about to let them both die without a fight.

Going low, she returned fire, her aim meant to warn and not kill. She emptied a handful of rounds, and the assailant's bullets stopped.

The motorcycle revved and tires screeched. Then, silence.

Keeping the gun ready, Maya emerged from her shelter. The shooter was gone. But for how long?

He could be reloading. Or looking for a better position to take them out.

Time to move.

Cash slumped against the side of the car, eyes closed. Tucking the Glock into her waistband, she jiggled his good shoulder. "Hey, you still with me? We gotta go."

No way could she carry him.

"Please, get up. Come on."

Blood trickled down the side of his head, and small cuts crossed his face.

"Cash." She shook him again.

A groan escaped his lips, but he stirred.

"Think you can make it to my car?"

He looked at her, eyes glazed, but nodded.

She helped him stand, easing herself under his shoulder again. With a few stumbles, they made it to her SUV. He fell into the passenger seat, and she shut the door, then ran to the driver's side.

No time to wait for help. They had to go before the shooter returned.

Speeding out of the industrial park, she kept watch for the

street bike. She dialed 911, then reported the incident and their location.

"I'm on my way to Memorial Hospital," she told the dispatcher. "With an injured GBI agent. ETA twenty minutes." Fifteen if she continued breaking the speed limit.

"I've alerted Pendleton PD," the dispatcher said. "Two squad cars are en route. They'll give you an escort."

Cash hadn't moved since she'd gotten him into the seat. At the stop sign, she reached over and pressed two fingers to his neck. Still beating. Still breathing.

God must have a sense of humor. Whatever she had expected to find out here at this time of night, it certainly wasn't Cash Brenner.

She brushed at tiny shards of glass stuck in his hair. A couple strands of silver peppered the hair at his temple, standing out in his dark brown locks. A few more since the last time she'd seen him, but he'd never seemed bothered by the early grays.

Headlights shone behind her. "That was fast."

"Excuse me?" the dispatcher answered.

"I see a vehicle approaching. Is that my escort?"

"Um…" Sounds of a keyboard clacking came over the line. "No, ma'am. Our guys are still a few miles away."

Was it the shooter? Two headlights. Not the motorcycle. Still… She sped up, but the vehicle kept pace.

"I think I'm being followed," she said.

"Where are you now?"

"Just past the intersection of Pine and Bellow Streets." It wasn't the first time she'd picked up a tail. In her line of work, it happened once in a while. "I'm going to see if I can lose them." She took a left turn, then a right. "No, still there."

"Can you give me a description of the vehicle?"

"It's dark. Looks like a sedan. Late model, I think."

The dispatcher's keys clicked again. "Okay, hold tight. Just a couple more blocks."

She glanced at Cash. His head fell forward, his chin resting on his chest.

Maya didn't have time to play cat and mouse.

The traffic signal ahead turned yellow. She floored it, making it through the intersection just as the light turned red.

"Okay," the dispatcher said. "You should see two PPD cruisers converging on your location."

Two silver police cars pulled up, red and blue lights flashing.

"Got 'em." She clicked her lights twice to acknowledge the officers. One car got in front of her, and the other fell in behind.

She checked her side mirror. The dark sedan had vanished. Maybe it was nothing. Or maybe whoever it was had been scared off by the police.

Maya thanked the dispatcher and clicked off the call. She let out a breath. "Hang on, Cash. We're almost there."

She followed the police cruiser to the emergency room entrance and hopped out. The hospital doors flew open, and they were surrounded by medical workers. Cash was loaded onto a gurney.

He mumbled something. Maya stepped closer.

"What is it, Cash?"

"Owen," he said, his voice weak. "Call…Owen."

Of course. Owen Donnelly was Cash's best friend and partner at the GBI.

"Got it." She couldn't help the ice in her tone. "Will do."

She'd hoped for at least a thank-you for saving his life.

But then again, she'd given up on Cash Brenner doing the right thing a long time ago.

Maya paced the hall outside the emergency department. When she'd called Owen and told him about Cash's accident, he'd asked her to wait for him to arrive. But staying in the sitting area had felt too much like she was a friend or family member waiting for information about a loved one.

She was neither to Cash. She'd tried stepping outside for some fresh air, but the dark parking lot had given her the creeps. The memory of the gunman had her jumping at shadows. Settling just inside the building where she could watch the entrance had felt like a better option.

The automatic doors opened, sending a warm breeze from the late spring weather inside. A couple strode in. Not Cash's partner. The sooner Owen got here, the sooner she could leave.

She undid the ponytail holding her long, wavy hair, combed her fingers through it, then pulled it back up. It was a habit of hers to do that when she was stressed.

Taking a seat on a bench, she took a long sip from the water bottle she'd brought with her, her mind churning over all that had happened tonight.

Cash Brenner. Why was he in Pendleton? He lived in Gadden Valley, almost an hour away. Seeing him again had brought up all kinds of feelings she'd rather not explore.

What was he doing in the industrial park? She had only been out there because she had followed a clue as to where her missing sister might be.

Her stomach tightened. *Jaida.* Her younger sister, whom she hadn't seen since Jaida was a year old. Maya had been nine when her sister was adopted out of foster care. Twenty years ago. She'd tried for years to find her sister, but to no avail. The adoption records had been sealed, and no one by the name Jaida Reid seemed to exist. Maya assumed the adoptive parents had changed her sister's name.

And then, three weeks ago, she'd received an email. Jaida, whose name was now Laurel DeWitt, had tracked her down. One of those DNA companies had matched their profiles. Maya had set up an account years ago in hopes of finding her sister, but nothing had turned up back then.

Laurel was a grad student at East Ridge University, less than an hour away. She had hoped to find her birth parents. But instead, she'd found Maya, the sister Laurel hadn't known existed. It seemed a clerical error had disconnected the two sisters, and Laurel's adoptive parents had been told she was an only child.

They had arranged to meet for lunch in East Ridge last week, but Maya had waited at the restaurant for two hours. Laurel never showed.

And now she was missing.

The doors opened again, and Owen hurried down the hall toward her. Maya had worried about waking him up at this late hour, but Owen was dressed in his GBI uniform. His sandy blond hair was combed into place, and his deep blue eyes were alert. "Thanks for waiting." He reached a hand out, and she shook it.

"No problem."

He nodded toward the ER. "Any word?"

"Um..." She swallowed. "I'm not...that is, I didn't, uh... leave my name."

"Oh. Right."

Heat rushed her cheeks, but if Owen noticed, he didn't say anything.

"Mind coming with me while I check?"

"Do you really need me?"

"I want to see my partner, and then I'd like for both of you to tell me what happened tonight."

She followed him through the doors to the registration desk. Owen asked for an update on Cash's condition.

"Are you family?" the nurse asked.

He flashed his badge. "His partner."

"Of course, sir. I'll have someone take you back."

They waited at the desk while the nurse made a call.

Owen stayed quiet, and Maya couldn't think of anything to say.

She'd met Cash's partner a couple times during the few

months they'd dated. But Cash hadn't stuck around long enough for her to know much about the guy.

"Cash Brenner family?" A young woman with short dark hair, wearing a white lab coat over blue scrubs, walked up.

"That's us." Owen stood. "Well, I'm his partner at the GBI. His emergency contact."

"I'm Dr. Abner." The woman turned to Maya. "And you are?"

"A friend," Owen answered for her, cutting off any protest. "How's Cash?"

Dr. Abner smiled. "He should be fine. We're treating him for a level three concussion, so we've moved him to a regular room to keep him for observation."

"Can we see him?" Owen asked.

We? How did she get roped into this?

"Sure," Dr. Abner said. "Follow me."

Owen motioned her forward.

Maya eyed the exit sign as they passed, wishing for a graceful way to retreat.

Cash leaned against the pillows, trying to find a comfortable position on the hospital bed. His left shoulder still hurt, but the pain had subsided to a dull ache. Having the doctor set the arm back into the socket had helped. So had the sling his arm was in now.

Too bad he was left-handed. It would be a challenge doing things with his right hand for a little while.

After getting a couple stitches for the cut over his brow, he'd been through several tests, including an MRI. He must've hit his head pretty hard when his car crashed because he couldn't remember anything before waking up in the emergency room. The doc called it a level three concussion but said it sounded worse than it was. Still, he had to stay in the hospital at least overnight.

He checked the clock on the wall. Almost 2 a.m. Not much

left of this night. He rubbed his good hand across his forehead, wishing he could wipe away the fuzziness in his mind. He wasn't even sure how he'd gotten to the hospital.

Or why Maya Reid's face kept popping into his mind. He hadn't seen her since their last date. The one where he'd realized he was falling for her. And known he had to walk away.

Cash had never let himself get close to anyone. Not in any real way. He'd seen enough of his mother's heartbreak every time his dad disappeared. He never wanted to feel like that or let someone else down in the same way. Especially not Maya. He had ended things with her before either of them got hurt. At least, that was what he told himself.

He let out a slow breath, trying to clear his mind of the swirling thoughts. His eyelids drooped. The lights were dimmed, and the pain meds they'd given him were starting to kick in. At least the three-ring circus going off in his head had calmed to a low roar.

A knock sounded at the door. Cash opened his eyes to see a nurse enter. She checked the machines at the head of his bed, then pulled a syringe from the pocket of her scrubs.

"What's that?" he asked.

"Just a little something to help you sleep." Her voice was muffled behind the mask she wore over her nose and mouth. A surgical cap covered her hair.

"I think I'll be able to sleep without it. I'm pretty tired."

"Doctor's orders." Her eyes crinkled. She must be smiling behind the mask.

Odd that she was wearing one. He tried to remember if the other attendants had.

The nurse reached for the IV port in his arm to insert the medication from the syringe. Cash glanced at her name tag.

"Thanks, Edith."

His eyes went to the tag again. The picture on the ID badge

was of a dark-skinned woman. But the woman next to him had fair skin.

"Wait!" He tried to sit up, but she pressed on his left shoulder. Pain shot through him, and he fell back with a grunt.

She stabbed the needle into his IV. He gripped her arm with his good hand. She struggled, but he was stronger. Pushing her away, he swung his legs over the side of the bed. The room spun, and he pitched forward.

His attacker came at him again, but he used his momentum to shove her back. She hit the small bed table, knocking a plastic pitcher of water to the floor. Darkness pulled at the edges of his vision. Sweat popped across his forehead.

He was going to pass out.

The door swung open.

"Excuse me? What are you doing?" He recognized the doctor with short dark hair from the ER. Dr. Abner.

The nurse shoved the bed table at the doctor, then fled out the door.

"What's going on?" Owen's voice reached him. His partner stepped into the room, followed by someone else.

Maya? He did a double take, his stomach flipping. What was she—

The doctor rushed over to Cash. "What happened?"

"Syringe. In the… IV." Cash's brain struggled to catch up.

Dr. Abner turned to Owen. "Get that nurse!"

The door slammed as Owen rushed out. The doctor pressed the emergency button on his bed rail, then began pulling out the IV.

Alarm spread through his chest as the room filled with nurses. Tubes were removed from his arm, machines turned off, and the doctor began checking his vitals.

"What…what did she give me?" Cash asked.

"I'm not sure, but I'm not taking any chances." She started to hand the syringe to a technician.

"Evidence," Cash said.

"Right." Dr. Abner grabbed a plastic bag and dropped the syringe in. "We'll save this for your partner." She turned to the tech. "Blood draw and full panel now. I want to know everything that's in his system."

A flurry of commotion ensued. At some point, Owen returned and took up post near the door. And Maya. She stood still in the corner of the room, eyes wide.

"Did you find her?" Dr. Abner asked Owen.

"She got away." Anger colored his tone. "I lost her somewhere around the third floor. I've got hospital security searching, and they've put the building on lockdown."

"Good," the doctor said. She patted Cash's arm. "I think you'll be okay, but we'll check everything to be sure."

"Guess it's a good thing we came in when we did." Owen turned to Maya.

Cash still couldn't believe she was here. And he didn't understand why. "What is going on?"

Maya turned incredulous eyes to him. "Cash, someone is trying to kill you."

TWO

"Kill me?" Cash's gaze bounced from Maya to Owen. "Why would someone want to kill me?"

"You don't know?" Owen's eyebrows rose.

"Should I?"

Owen exchanged a look with Maya, concern etched on both their faces. Cash still didn't understand what Maya was doing in his hospital room or what she and Owen seemed to be keeping from him.

He was tired, hurting and confused.

Frustration built. "Someone needs to tell me what's going on. Now."

Owen sighed, then stepped closer to the bed. "Where were you tonight?"

"I was—" His mind was blank. Why didn't he have an answer? "I…was in a car accident…right?" He looked at Owen for confirmation.

But his partner's mouth pressed into a thin line. "You were."

Dr. Abner spoke up. "Cash, can you tell me what happened to cause you to crash?"

"Um…" Cash searched for the answer, but it was like a big, black curtain had been pulled across his mind. "I…was driving. And…" He tried to remember, but all that came to him was a vision of lights coming at him and then pain. He recalled what he'd heard in the ER. "I hit a tree. Someone cut me off and ran me off the road."

Maya stepped closer, her eyes wide. "Is that what you remember?"

"At this moment, yes. Why? Is that not what happened?"

She tilted her head, eyes narrowed. "You ran into me."

"I did?" That didn't make any sense. "Is that why you're here?" Was she hurt, too?

"I'm here because after I scared off some guy on a motorcycle shooting at us, I thought it best to get us both out of there and get you some medical help." Sarcasm dripped from her tone.

How could he not remember any of that? He had so many questions.

Owen held up a hand before he could ask any of them. "Wait, someone shot at both of you?"

"What were we doing together?" he asked.

A hint of red rose in her cheeks. "We weren't together. I was leaving the industrial park. Your Mustang came out of nowhere, almost clipped my front fender and crashed into the trees. You got out of the car, clearly injured. Before I could do much to help, a black street bike pulled up and the guy started shooting."

Owen turned to him. "Cash, you called me around midnight. Said you were in Pendleton, but the call kept cutting out. You said you found something. Then I heard a gunshot and the line went dead. Do you remember any of that? Where you were or what you were doing?"

Cash closed his eyes, trying to think back. But again, only a blank space where the answer should be. He rubbed his good hand across his forehead.

"Just relax." Dr. Abner spoke in a quiet, calm tone. "Take some slow, deep breaths. Now, what is the last thing you remember before the accident?"

He did as she said, leaning back into the pillows, willing his mind to work. "I was at home. Had dinner. Was working in my garage. On the hot rod."

The 1970 Mustang Mach 1 he'd picked up at an auction was in bad shape, but tinkering with it was one of his favorite ways to spend his off hours.

"And then what?" Dr. Abner said. "You got in the car. Where did you go?"

Cash tried, but he came up empty. He sat up, slamming his fist into the bed. "I don't remember!"

"Okay, okay." Pressing his good shoulder, she gently eased him back to the pillows. She tapped on the tablet in her hand.

"What does that mean?" he asked. "Why can't I remember?" Panic began to spread across his chest.

"Temporary memory loss is fairly common after an injury like yours."

"How temporary is it?" Owen asked.

"Usually, memories return in a few days. Rest will help. I'll run a few more tests to make sure there's not something serious going on."

He looked at Owen. "Maybe then I'll remember why someone tried to kill me." He felt exposed, helpless. It was unnerving.

And he wanted it to go away. Immediately.

"I have more questions," Owen said, turning to Maya. "You said you scared off the shooter. How did you do that?"

As she explained how she'd pushed Cash to safety and used his gun to fire back at their assailant, he had to remind himself not to stare at her with his mouth open.

Maya was no wilting flower. She'd been through hard times as a foster child. It had made her strong, tough. Brave.

He could never guess his own life would depend on her courage or skills.

After the way he'd treated her, he didn't deserve that. Not from her.

But he wasn't the same man she'd known two years ago. He had given his life to Christ last year, and it had changed him.

"Do you think the shooter followed you to the hospital?" Owen asked her.

"It's possible." Maya's brows pulled together. "I thought I had a tail on the way here, but they disappeared when the PPD showed up."

Which meant one of two things. Either the shooter was the woman posing as a nurse. Or there were two of them, working in tandem. And they had both gotten a good look at Maya, putting her in possible danger as well.

Owen pulled his phone from his pocket. "I called SAC Overstreet on my way here. He should be arriving any minute."

Layton Overstreet was the Special Agent in Charge of their GBI field office. Between him and Owen, they would pull in their entire team at the Appalachian Investigations Division.

"We'll set up a watch schedule," Owen said to Dr. Abner. "We'd like to keep a team member in this room at all times."

Great. Now he needed babysitting.

"Is that necessary?" Cash asked.

Owen shot him a dark look. "From what I just witnessed, I'd say yes."

"All right," Dr. Abner said. "Your vitals look good. I'm going to check on your blood work." She handed Owen the bag with the syringe. "I'm sure you'll want to check this for fingerprints."

"I doubt you'll find any," Cash said. "She was wearing gloves."

"Maybe we'll catch a break." Owen stepped to the door with Dr. Abner. "I'll talk to Overstreet, and then I want to check in with security to see if they've found anything." Owen shot a glance at Maya before walking out.

Cash thought he noticed an almost imperceptible nod from her. What was that about?

Maya watched the door close behind Owen as if she were watching the last lifeboat of the Titanic sail away without her.

Arms crossed, she shifted from one foot to the other as tension filled the room.

She was so beautiful. He hadn't forgotten, but seeing her again, he was struck by her beauty anyway.

Jet black hair pulled away from the soft lines of her face. Smooth, olive skin. Her eyes, deep brown with flecks of amber, darted around the room, looking anywhere but at him.

She obviously wanted to go, yet she stayed.

And he realized why.

She wouldn't leave him unguarded.

Not with Owen gone. She was watching out for him.

He would be dead if it weren't for her.

"Thank you." He tried to keep his tone light, but his throat constricted. "For saving my life."

Maya wasn't prepared for the flood of emotions that washed over her. The adrenaline from earlier had faded. She had gone into defense mode when the assailant on the bike had shot at them. Fight-or-flight had turned into fear when they'd found Cash being attacked in his hospital room.

Now she wasn't sure how to feel. Cash's gratitude, his honest vulnerability, was more frightening than a bullet.

And almost as deadly.

She couldn't afford to be pulled in again, no matter how much she wanted to cross the room and smooth the worry from his brow.

"You're welcome," she managed.

"So, what were you doing at the industrial park so late?" He gave her a friendly smile. "I have to ask."

Of course. She'd wondered when that would come up. "I was working on a case, actually."

"Still doing the P.I. thing?"

Her profession sometimes put her on the outs with local law enforcement. Private investigators trod the fine line between citizen and police.

Cash had never seemed bothered by what she did for a living.

"Yes," Maya said. "A missing person."

"Oh?" He sat up, his attention spurred. "Care to share?"

She hesitated. The last two years had been spent trying to forget Cash. In the few months they'd dated, she had found Cash to be a great sounding board for when she was stuck on a case. She was usually guarded with others, especially about personal details, but she'd gotten closer to him, opened up to him, more than she had with anyone else in her life.

Growing up in the foster system hadn't given her the chance to connect with many people. There were even fewer that she trusted. But she had felt something with Cash. And it wasn't just because of his good looks. He seemed to understand her on a deeper level. Made her feel truly seen.

Until he'd walked away. No explanation. She hadn't hurt like that in a long time. But Cash's vulnerability tonight broke down her defenses. She explained what had happened with Laurel.

"I remember you mentioning your sister who was adopted. Amazing that you found each other after all this time."

She had shared her frustrations with Cash once when she'd reached another dead end in the search for Laurel. He had been supportive and encouraging. Two weeks later, he'd ended their relationship.

As if reading her thoughts, he frowned and shook his head. "Sorry." He cleared his throat. "So, she didn't show up for lunch. Could she have forgotten?"

"I doubt it. She sounded so excited to meet up. We made plans the week before, but I didn't think I'd need to confirm again." She'd wondered if Laurel had changed her mind about meeting the sister she'd never known she had.

"I know it's obvious, but have you tried calling?"

She nodded. "And texting and calling some more. Her number goes straight to voice mail. I even got her address and went to her apartment."

"And nothing?"

"Not much. Her roommate was home. Skylar Hudson. She said Laurel had left the week before to go stay with her boyfriend and hadn't returned home."

"Was this her usual behavior?"

"I mean, I've never actually met her, so I have no idea. Skylar didn't seem to think it was a big deal."

Cash shrugged. "Well, maybe it's not."

She chewed her bottom lip. Should she tell him the rest? Holding back details wouldn't help her find her sister. "There's something else. Skylar said Laurel had…a drug problem." She cringed inwardly just saying it out loud.

"What kind of drugs?"

"Prescription painkillers. I think it started from an injury and then got worse. Apparently, she's been flunking out of grad school because of it."

Cash sighed and closed his eyes. When he opened them again, his expression was full of sympathy. "I'm sorry. That's awful."

She nodded, the lump in her throat cutting off words. Maya and her sister had been put into foster care after their mother died from an overdose. The fact that her sister now had an addiction cut deep.

"So, what makes you think she's missing?" Cash asked.

"A couple of things don't add up. Laurel is a grad student at East Ridge. From what I found, she has been an excellent student, even making the dean's list last semester. She doesn't seem like someone who has a drug problem. And if she does, it's very new. Plus, she seemed so excited to meet me. Why would she take off to her boyfriend's right after making plans with me?"

"Have you checked with her boyfriend?"

She shook her head. "Skylar only knew his first name and no address. Apparently, it's also a new development."

"Well, so far, all of these things are plausible. What about her parents? Have you checked with them?"

"I tried. Their housekeeper said they were out of town."

"And not worried that their daughter is MIA?"

"So far, I seem to be the only one." She was probably making a bigger deal out of it than it was, but she couldn't shake the feeling that something was wrong. "But they should be back by now. I plan to pay them a visit tomorrow."

Maybe if she could look her sister's adoptive parents in the eye, she could get a better read on things.

"Okay," Cash said. "How does this tie in with you being at the industrial park tonight?"

Heat rose in her cheeks again. This was where she could go from concerned sister to all-out stalker. But she was already in this far, and she had a feeling Cash wasn't going to let it go.

"I saw a picture. On her social media. She likes to take pictures of squirrels and post them. The last picture she posted was a couple of weeks before she called me. It was of a squirrel sitting on top of a trash can, eating a nut. There was a building in the background. Lazer Industries. They have an office building in the industrial park."

"I see. So, you went there to check it out."

She nodded.

"Find anything?"

"No. No one there claims to have ever seen Laurel."

"No one who was there at, say, midnight?" He quirked an eyebrow at her.

Busted. She dropped her eyes to the floor. "I went back after hours tonight to snoop around."

"Of course you did."

She raised her gaze to meet Cash's, but his face was kind.

"I'm sorry. Maybe once I get out of here, we could look into it for you. It actually reminds me of—"

Cash's thought was cut off as SAC Overstreet strode into Cash's hospital room followed by Owen. Both men wore stern expressions.

"Boss." Cash sat up a little straighter in his hospital bed.

As the Special Agent in Charge of their team, Layton Overstreet struck an imposing figure. Tall and broad, with a little extra weight around his middle, and curly black hair that he kept trimmed military style.

Around the office, he was known as The Bear. He commanded respect, but he would walk through fire for any of his team. And they all knew it.

His dark eyes scanned Cash, and then he rested a hand on each hip. "How you doing, son?"

Cash tried to shrug off the concern. "A little banged up, but not too bad. Could've been worse."

Overstreet's eyes narrowed. He nodded and turned to Maya. "But it wasn't, thanks to you." He stuck out a hand. "Layton Overstreet."

She returned the shake, her hand swallowed up in Overstreet's large one. "Maya Reid."

"Agent Donnelly tells me you're a private investigator."

"Yes, sir."

"And that's how you came to be in the industrial park tonight?"

"Actually," Cash spoke up. "Maya was just telling me about the case she's working. I think it might be something you both should hear about."

"Oh?" Overstreet raised a bushy eyebrow.

Cash nodded encouragement to Maya, and she repeated the information about her missing sister.

Owen turned to Cash. "You know what this reminds me of." His eyes softened.

Cash nodded, his pulse spiking.

"The Fielding case," Overstreet said, finishing their thoughts.

Everyone on their team knew it was Cash's living nightmare. The case he couldn't shake.

Elizabeth Fielding had disappeared from East Ridge University four years ago. A straight A student who volunteered at a homeless shelter. Vanished without a trace.

Elizabeth's body had never been found. And no closure given to her family.

He didn't want that for Maya.

The similarities to her missing sister bothered him. A grad student. Missing from East Ridge. With evidence of drug abuse. And something else he couldn't quite put his finger on.

"Cash," Owen said. "You're always working on the Fielding case in your spare time. Could that be what you were doing tonight?"

He tried to remember but nothing surfaced. "I have no idea." It made his head hurt to try to think through it.

"There could be a connection here," Overstreet said. "Wouldn't hurt to look into it." He turned to Maya. "Why don't you come by our office tomorrow afternoon? I'd like the other team members to hear about this as well."

"I…uh…" Maya's eyes widened, and she glanced between the three of them, landing on Cash for a moment.

She didn't want to work with him. The realization hit like a rock in his gut.

He had hurt her. The one thing he had tried to avoid. Breaking up with her had been a way to protect her. Or maybe he had only been trying to protect himself.

Shame fell over him. He knew God had forgiven him, but he still had much to make up for when it came to the broken hearts he had left in his wake.

"I really think we could help." He hoped his quiet tone and imploring expression conveyed how he felt. "Please, let us."

Doubt wavered in her eyes for a moment, but she took a breath and nodded. "All right. I can do that."

"Great," Overstreet said. "We'll see you tomorrow afternoon. And…thank you. For looking out for my guy. You're quite the hero, I hear."

Her gaze dropped to the floor. "Just doing what anyone else would've done in the situation." She had never been comfortable accepting compliments.

"I could argue that point." He turned to Cash. "But for now, let's focus on finding out who's after you, Brenner."

"I wish I knew."

Overstreet crossed his arms across his chest. "All right, let's start with what we do know."

As Owen and Maya went through their version of what had happened, Cash searched his memory for anything to connect to what they were saying. But he came up empty.

It was like listening to someone talk about a movie they'd seen. He couldn't picture it, and he felt completely disconnected.

"And you don't remember where you were or what happened before you ran into Miss Reid?" Overstreet asked.

"No, sir." He didn't even remember why he'd left home tonight.

"Okay," Owen said. "Let's reverse engineer this. You said you found something. If it wasn't the Fielding case, I'm assuming it was for one of your other cases. Any of them connected to Pendleton?"

Cash went through the list of open cases in his mind, but nothing jumped out at him. "I don't think so." How could he remember those so clearly but not what he was doing a few hours ago?

"If it was about one of your cases, I would think you'd call your partner." Overstreet speared him with a look.

Now it was Cash's turn to look at the floor. He had a reputation as being a bit impulsive, not always following the rules or chain of command. Especially if it meant closing a case.

But he also had the highest close rate of anyone in their office, and Overstreet trusted him. He had allowed Cash a wide berth when it came to the restraints of procedure. Nothing that would get either of them fired, but he also didn't make Cash walk a tight line. He knew Cash would do whatever it took to stop the bad guys.

Had a reckless decision led to this?

"What about your phone?" Maya said. "We could check the history. See if anything links to what you were up to."

"Good idea." Owen went to the small closet and pulled out the bag with the clothes Cash had been wearing when he'd arrived at the hospital. "Here it is."

Cash took the phone and unlocked it with his thumbprint, then scrolled through the texts. "Nothing weird here."

"What about phone calls?"

He checked. "Yeah, one from an unknown number. Came in around ten thirty p.m." He dialed, but the number rang and rang. "No answer."

"Could be a burner." Overstreet reached for the phone and copied the number. "I'll get Agent Chandler on this first thing."

Noah Chandler, a new agent in their office, specialized in computer forensics.

"We can also get him to see where Cash's phone pinged when he called me," Owen said.

"Maybe that will help jog my memory." Cash hated this feeling of not knowing.

Overstreet stepped to his bedside. "We'll figure it out. For now, try to get some rest."

"The doc said that would help your memories," Owen said. "And I'm staying here, taking first shift tonight."

Cash also hated feeling helpless.

"I should probably head out," Maya said.

"Of course," Overstreet said. "You've had a long night. We'll talk tomorrow. Thank you, once again, for your help."

The threats were aimed at him, but Cash didn't like the idea of Maya being left alone. He caught Owen's eye, and his partner nodded.

"Agent King is standing by to escort you home," he said.

Agent Addie King was another member of their unit. And one of the nicest people Cash had ever known.

"I don't think that's necessary," Maya said.

"Maybe not." Overstreet gave her a polite smile. "But let's err on the side of caution."

The SAC had a way of silencing any arguments. With a final nod, they left.

Owen settled in a chair near the door. "All right, you heard the man. Get some shut-eye."

Cash doubted the assailant would try another attack tonight, now that they were alerted to the threat. But maybe the doc was right. He would do whatever it took to get his memory back. Because until he knew who was after him and why, he would be sleeping with one eye open.

THREE

Maya drove down the freeway at an easy pace the following afternoon. Traffic into Atlanta was light this time of day, thankfully. Laurel's parents were back in town. She had confirmed it with the housekeeper yesterday. It was time to meet them face-to-face.

She sipped the last of the organic black tea in her insulated thermos. She preferred it over coffee. Now she wished she'd brought an extra. She yawned. After crawling into bed in the early morning hours, she'd tossed and turned, her mind circling on all that had happened the night before. And seeing Cash again. She had finally given up on sleep and started her day around nine.

Checking in with Cash crossed her mind, but she pushed the thought away. He had seemed sincere when offering to help. And it had felt so natural to fall back into their rhythm of bouncing ideas off each other about a case. She had been fooled by Cash before, though, and she had to keep her wits about her when it came to him.

SAC Overstreet had asked her to meet with him later this afternoon. The two cases and their similarities intrigued her. But working with the GBI, or any team, was hard to wrap her mind around. Her childhood had taught her to depend on no one except herself.

First, she needed to see the DeWitts. The urgent need to find her sister overrode everything else.

She took the exit toward Orchard Park, a ritzy suburb on the northern outskirts of Atlanta. The upscale neighborhood was a private oasis close enough to the city for easy commutes but far enough away to allow for large estates and plenty of green space. Carefully manicured lawns and flower gardens bordered brick and stucco homes that Maya guessed would carry million-dollar price tags.

Reaching the DeWitts' address, she pulled into the circular driveway that led up to the two-story brick home. From her research, she'd learned Wade and Helene DeWitt owned a large export trading company and had been very successful over the years. Laurel was listed as their only child.

What must it have been like to grow up in a place like this? She tucked the thought away and got out of her vehicle, took the six steps up to the grand front door, and rang the bell.

Half expecting to see a butler in a full tuxedo open the door, she was surprised to see a red-haired woman in cream-colored slacks and a lavender sweater.

Her hazel-green eyes roamed over Maya. "May I help you?"

Not a match for the picture she'd seen of Helene DeWitt on the company's website. And probably not the housekeeper she'd spoken to on the phone, who had a noticeably thick, German accent.

"I'd like to speak to Mr. and Mrs. DeWitt."

"And you are…?"

"I'm…looking for their daughter." Until she knew who this woman was, Maya wasn't about to divulge her life story.

The woman's eyes narrowed. "Who sent you? Who are you working with? *The Metropolitan Journal?* Or maybe *The Observer*?"

"I'm not a reporter. I'm an investigator."

One perfectly shaped eyebrow rose at her.

Fine. She promised herself she would do whatever it took to find Maya. Even if it meant dealing with Cash. "Working with the GBI."

The woman's eyes widened, and she pressed a hand to her chest. "Oh, my."

When she didn't move out of the doorway, Maya prompted, "May I come in, Miss…?"

She blinked. "Oh, of course. I'm sorry." She opened the door wider and stepped back. "Audra Peterson, Mr. DeWitt's executive assistant."

Maya entered the two-story foyer with marble-tiled floors and a chandelier hanging overhead. *Wow.* She pulled her eyes away and focused on Miss Peterson. "Are the DeWitts at home?"

"Yes, but…" She pressed her lips together, looking down the hallway toward the rear of the house.

"But?"

"Only that…they're a bit occupied at the moment. They're hosting an event here this evening, and well…you see, this isn't a good time for—"

"For discussing the whereabouts of their daughter?" Maya hadn't come all this way to be put off again.

"What's this about my daughter?" A petite woman came around the corner carrying a large vase filled with flowers.

Maya recognized Helene DeWitt. Her research had listed the woman's age as barely over fifty, but in person, she looked much younger. Probably had tons of facelifts and expensive skin treatments to thank for that.

She was dressed in a light pink blouse and a long floral skirt. Her honey-blond hair was swept into a low ponytail.

Her blue eyes seemed to brighten as she approached Maya. "You have information about Laurel?"

"I was hoping you would have information for me," Maya said.

"She's with the GBI," Miss Peterson said.

Helene handed the vase to the assistant. "Audra, take these and go find Wade. Have him meet us in the parlor."

"Yes, ma'am." Audra took the flowers and disappeared down the hall.

"This way." Helene motioned for Maya to follow her across the foyer and into another large room. A marble fireplace was centered along the wall between oak bookshelves that reached the ceiling.

Helene took a seat on a beige sofa and motioned for Maya to join her.

"I'm sorry about all the commotion." Her hands flitted in a gesture that reminded Maya of a butterfly's wings. "We're hosting a dinner tonight for our board of directors and some investors. We've had caterers and florists and technicians traipsing in and out of here all day."

Not the picture Maya had expected to find. How could they be hosting some dinner when Laurel was missing? Did they not care that their daughter had disappeared?

The door at the other end of the room opened. A man with salt-and-pepper hair and deep brown eyes strode across the thick carpet. Even in his casual khakis and navy polo shirt, Wade DeWitt exuded authority and wealth.

"You're with the GBI?" He didn't waste time with introductions.

Maya stood and faced him. "Yes." She hoped he didn't ask to see a badge.

Wade rested both hands at his hips. "And what it is you want to know about Laurel?"

The questions she had prepared fled from her mind. The man was intimidating. It was easy to see why he'd found success in running a multimillion-dollar company.

She glanced to the left and noticed a picture of Laurel on a side table. Her beautiful sister. Blonde with blue eyes, she looked a bit like Helene. But she was the very image of their mother, Valerie. Before her addiction had destroyed her life and wrecked her family. And separated her daughters.

She squared her shoulders. “When was the last time you spoke with your daughter?”

“Four weeks ago.” Helene spoke from her spot on the sofa. “Right before we left for Italy.”

“And you haven’t spoken to her since?”

She shook her head.

“Have you tried contacting her?”

“Yes, but she hasn’t returned any of my calls or texts.” Her eyes dropped to the floor. She clasped her hands together in her lap.

Maya took a seat next to her again and softened her tone. “Is this normal behavior?”

“No.” Helene raised her head, worry showing in her eyes. “We used to speak every few days until—”

“Helene.” Wade’s tone indicated his wife should stop talking.

“Until what?” Maya asked, glancing from Helene to Wade.

His mouth cut a thin line.

“I’ve already spoken with Laurel’s roommate,” Maya said. “She told me about the drug problem.”

Something between a sigh and a sob came from Helene.

Wade’s face turned even harder. “Then you know,” he said.

“Know what?”

“What she’s become.”

“Someone with an addiction?”

“Just like her mother,” he said between gritted teeth.

“Her mother?” Anger pooled in her stomach. How dare he talk about their mother?

But Helene pressed a hand to her arm. “Laurel was adopted. Her mother died from an overdose when Laurel was a baby.”

“Oh?” Maya feigned surprise. She hadn’t told them who she was for a number of reasons. An investigator working on a case was more likely to get information from them than a sister who wasn't also adopted by this family. Or any other.

And that was the second reason. She regarded these two people who had taken her sister into their family and given her the kind of home Maya could only dream of, and the opportunities that came with a life like this.

It was a reminder of what she'd never had. Of what she could never have. A family. Parents who loved her. Wanted her.

Now she wondered what kind of life her sister had led in this house. With these people who didn't seem to care if she ever came home again.

Wade ran a hand down his face. "Look, we didn't know, all right? We didn't know about the drugs. If we had, we would've—" He shook his head. "Regardless, the fact is, Laurel has a problem. And now she's run off with her dopehead friends. And I can't—" He stepped closer. "I can't have a media circus camped out on my front lawn. Not now. I'm in the middle of a very important business deal, and I can't have this story running in every newspaper in town."

Maya couldn't believe her ears. "Are you saying you don't even want me to look for your daughter?"

"No. I didn't mean that. I—" He sighed. "Look for her. Just… keep it under the radar."

"Sir?" The assistant, Audra, stepped into the room. She glanced from Wade to Helene to Maya. "I'm sorry, sir, but the mayor is on the phone. Something about a conflict for tonight."

"Great. That's all I need right now." Wade started to leave, then turned back to Maya, pointing a finger in her direction. "Remember what I said. No media coverage."

Cash drummed his fingers on the table in the break room of the GBI's field office. Having gotten released from the hospital after lunch, he'd coerced Owen into bringing him here.

He wanted to be around when Maya came in to talk to SAC Overstreet.

He and Owen had settled into the break room for coffee. He eyed the brown liquid in the mug in front of him. Decaf was a waste of coffee, in his opinion. But the doc had told him to limit his caffeine intake for a few days.

Dr. Abner had given him a clean bill of health. Physically, at least. The concussion and shoulder would heal soon. But he still couldn't remember where he'd been or what he'd been doing the night before. She speculated that his memory loss was more psychological than physical. Something tied to the trauma of the accident. Rest and time should help with that, too, she'd said.

He and Owen had spent the morning digging through his open case files, but nothing had triggered his memory. All he could think about was Maya and her missing sister.

She had told him yesterday that she was going to visit Laurel's parents, but then she hadn't shown up to meet with Overstreet. Was the idea of working with him so disgusting that she would decline the GBI's offer of help to find Laurel? He hated to think so.

He checked his phone. No messages.

Owen slapped his palm down on the table.

Cash sat up, focusing on his partner. "What?"

The last thing he'd heard Owen say was something about the ball game he planned to watch this weekend.

"Would you relax?" Owen eyed him, then smirked. "It's not like you're waiting for a date."

Cash glared, resisting the urge to kick his partner under the table. Owen hadn't left his side since the incident in the hospital. He was starting to feel like a watched pot waiting to boil.

He couldn't be angry at his partner. If the roles were reversed, he would do the same thing. Someone had tried to kill him. And he had no idea who or why.

His anger was at himself. At his mind for hiding his memories from him. If only he could remember what he was doing at the industrial park. But whenever he tried to recall the events of last night, his mind only returned blanks. Darkness. And nothing more.

His phone buzzed and he grabbed it, hoping to see a text from Maya that she was on her way. But it was only an email notification.

He sighed and stuffed the phone back into his pocket.

"Not from Maya?" Owen asked.

Cash shook his head. Where could she be?

Owen leaned forward, resting his elbows on the table. "So, what happened with you two?"

Cash took a long gulp of the coffee.

He hadn't told Owen the details of his breakup with Maya. Or, his lack of breakup. But nothing would be gained by keeping it to himself anymore. If they were going to be working together, he might as well come clean. "I ghosted her."

"Of course, you did." Owen rolled his eyes. "And after how long?"

"We went out for a few months." It was Cash's dating MO back then. He'd meet someone, go out a few times. But the moment he got the idea she wanted to get serious, he would go dark. Stop calling. Stop answering calls. Drop all communication until she got the idea it was over. Or, he'd offer a lame excuse about being busy with work or the time not being right for them.

At least, that had been his behavior before. Since becoming a Christian last year, he'd worked to overcome his fear of opening his heart to someone. But he wasn't there yet. The scars from his parents' miserable marriage ran deep. He'd found it easier to cut the possibility of a relationship out of the picture all together. Better for everyone than to risk hurting someone else the way he had Maya.

She'd been so great to be around. Strong, independent, fun.

The problem was Cash. He'd been the one to look for excuses to be around her. Think about her during quiet moments in the day. Wonder what she was doing. Pick up the phone a dozen times to call her but then question if she wanted to talk to him.

For the first time, he had been the one falling for her.

And that had terrified him more than anything had in a long time.

He shrugged. "We were just…not a good fit."

Owen raised an eyebrow, clearly seeing through the excuse. But thankfully, he didn't push.

"Why don't you call her and see where she is?" Owen said. "Maybe she forgot about the meeting?"

Maya wouldn't forget. And unless she had changed in the past two years, she wasn't the kind of person to promise to be somewhere and not show up.

Cash pulled out his phone, his thumb hovering over her name in his contacts. He'd never been able to delete it, even after two years. Calling Maya brought back the memory of their dates. But this was different. It was a business meeting. They were working on a case.

And he could be professional.

He pressed the call button. The line rang four times, then went to voice mail. He left a quick message, making sure to mention that both he and Owen were at the office for their meeting, and for her to call when she could.

If Maya was standing him up, he deserved it. But he couldn't push past the worry that something else was going on.

She had been with him when someone tried to kill him. Twice.

The feeling in his gut grew.

He stood, dumping his coffee into the sink. "I'm going to see Noah."

"To track her phone?"

"I..." How could he explain his need to check up on Maya? It barely made any sense to him either. "I need to know she's okay."

Maya headed for the door, anger pooling in her stomach at Wade's dismissal of his daughter's disappearance. He was more concerned for his reputation and profits than the well-being of his only child.

Helene hurried after her. "He's not usually like this. Please don't think him a monster. He is worried about Laurel. He's dealing with a lot right now. The stress of this acquisition and then Laurel's addiction...it's been too much."

Call her callous, but Maya found it hard to muster any sympathy for the millionaire.

"I should be going." She stepped outside.

"I'm sorry, dear, I didn't even get your name."

"It's Maya. Maya Reid."

Helene's perfectly shaped eyebrows rose. "Maya? You're... you're her, aren't you? Laurel's sister?"

"You know?" Maya stiffened.

"Laurel told me about locating you through that genealogy company. Oh, my dear!" She pulled Maya into a hug, holding on as if she were a lifelinc.

Unsure of how to react, she patted Helene awkwardly on the back, then stepped away to extricate herself from the embrace.

Helene's eyes glistened with tears. "You don't know what it meant to Laurel, to all of us, to find out she had a sister. I wish we'd known before." She regarded Maya. "You look so different, and yet, I can see some similarities. The shape of your nose, certain facial expressions."

"I look like our dad. Laurel took after our mom." In more than just her looks, it would appear. Addiction disorders were sometimes genetic. She had hoped both she and her sister had missed that trait. It didn't appear that Laurel had.

"Wait one moment." Helene walked over to a table in the foyer and opened a drawer, taking out a pad and pen. She scribbled something down, then returned to Maya. "This is my number. And this is the name of the young man Laurel is dating. Perhaps he might know where she is."

Maya read the name. Dillon Cordell. Skylar had told her his first name, but it would be easier to trace him with his full name. At least she now had more information than she'd had when she got here. "Thank you."

"Mrs. DeWitt?" Audra called from the dining room. "The florist has a question about the table arrangements."

"Of course. I'll be right there." Helene grasped Maya's hands. "Please, bring our girl home."

Her throat tight, Maya nodded and left. She climbed into her SUV and took a deep breath before putting the vehicle into Drive.

Thoughts and emotions swirled in her mind as she headed back to the freeway and turned north toward Gadden Valley. Her phone showed a couple of missed calls and a text from Cash. The visit had taken longer than she'd planned, and she had missed the meeting with SAC Overstreet, but at least she had a lead they could follow up on now.

Dillon Cordell. As soon as she got back, she would start her research and see what could be found on the young man her sister had been seeing. Interesting that Laurel's mother knew his full name but the roommate, Skylar, didn't.

Then again, just because two people were roommates didn't mean they were best friends. Laurel may not have shared everything with Skylar.

Or maybe Skylar had been holding out, and she knew more than she was admitting.

There was another lead she could share with Cash's team.

Images of Cash disturbed her train of thought. He had seemed sincere about their working together.

She recalled how he'd looked after the accident and in the hospital. Injured and bleeding, and then the confusion when he couldn't remember what had happened.

Careful. The last thing she needed was to start feeling sympathy for Cash. That was too close to forgiving. And forgiveness was a slippery slope.

She knew she was supposed to forgive. One of her foster parents, Mrs. Walker, had taught her the prayer about forgiving others as she had been forgiven. The same woman had led Maya to accept Christ into her heart.

But Maya's relationship with God was a complicated and troubled one. She believed in God. Yet, she couldn't quite grasp the idea of this unconditional love He was supposed to have for her. In foster care, she'd learned love was given to the good, the pretty, and the ones who did everything right. It wasn't given to the troublemakers. The ones who fought as a way of survival and didn't conform to someone else's idea of worthy.

The screeching of tires had her checking the rearview mirror. A box truck swerved around two cars and into the lane behind her. *Ugh.* Aggressive drivers were one of her pet peeves.

She was almost at her exit, so she clicked on her blinker and merged off the freeway onto the exit ramp. The truck followed. *Great.*

Maya turned right and headed down the two-lane road. The truck continued on the same route. Was she going to have to deal with this guy all the way into Gadden Valley?

The truck sped up, getting too close for comfort. Maya increased her speed, but the truck stayed on her tail.

Couldn't be road rage. She hadn't cut him off on the freeway. A slice of fear traveled down her spine as the truck became more aggressive. Was it the same person from last night?

The area became more rural and the road curvier the farther from the freeway they went. Farmland and pastures spread out on either side of the road. The truck's motor revved as it loomed behind her. Maybe she should call for help? She reached for her phone in the holder on her dash, but a sudden jolt shuddered through the car, jerking her hand away.

The truck had hit her bumper. And he was coming back for more.

Maya sped up, but she was no match for the truck. He rammed her again, and she held tight to the steering wheel as her car veered off the shoulder. She corrected and pulled her SUV into the lane again, only to be hit again.

Up ahead, the bridge over Coley Lake came into view. *Oh no.* If he hit her again, she could go over the side. She pressed her gas pedal down as far as it would go, but the truck kept coming.

Another hit, then a loud pop. Her car swerved wildly to the right. Her tire had blown! Maya struggled to control the vehicle, but it went into a spin. Her hands slipped from the wheel as the SUV hit the guardrail and flipped over it.

Maya shut her eyes as the car plunged over the side.

FOUR

Panic rose as Maya's vehicle hit the water. The airbag had deployed when she'd slammed into the guardrail. As it began to deflate, she could see the water rapidly floating towards the windows.

She took a mental inventory. Did she have any broken bones? It was hard to tell as adrenaline coursed through her body. She tried to recall her emergency training and how to escape a sinking car. Step one was... *What is step one?*

Taking a breath, she tried to calm down. It wouldn't help her situation if she gave in to the fear.

Get loose. That was it. Her fingers shook as she grabbed at the seat belt. Finally finding the latch, she unbuckled it. Her body fell forward as gravity began to pull the car down, and she braced against the steering wheel.

Dark water lapped against the windows. The heavy SUV was sinking fast. She tried not to focus on that or the water seeping into the cab from the floorboard.

Step two. Get the windows down before the electrical circuits shorted out. If the water rose above the windows, the pressure would make it almost impossible to roll them down. She pressed the automatic window button on her door panel. Water rushed inside, pushing her further into the car's interior.

No, no! She wanted out. Briny water filled her nose and mouth. Straining, she found an air pocket near the roof and gulped a breath. She tried pushing her way through the window opening, but the current was too strong.

Murky water began filling the interior as the vehicle sank beneath the surface.

Trapped. The desperation to pray filled her mind. Would God hear? No time to wonder.

God, please don't let me die. She had to find Laurel. Had to make sure her sister was safe.

Her lungs ached for air. Darkness pulled at the edges of her consciousness. Heaviness filled her limbs.

Something grabbed and pulled at her. She struggled against it, but it was too powerful. Then she was moving. Toward the light.

She broke through the surface, and oxygen flooded her lungs as she took a breath. She would never take breathing for granted again.

To her right, Cash's face came into view. His dark hair was soaked, and water dripped from his face. "Can you swim?"

Could she? The cold water made her muscles feel ten times heavier, and she worked to move her arms and legs, pushing against the waves.

"Come on," he said. "I've got you."

He wrapped an arm around her waist and began towing her to the shore.

The rear bumper of her SUV descended into the water, and then it was gone.

Shivers racked her body as they reached the shore, and Owen helped Cash pull her out of the water.

She sat with her elbows on her knees. Would she ever get enough air? She inhaled and coughed up the water lodged in her throat and lungs.

"Take slow breaths," Owen said.

She tried to follow his instructions, even though her body wanted to rebel.

"I got her," Cash said as he settled down next to her. A coat was thrown over her shoulders, and she relished the warmth.

Owen disappeared. Maya's thoughts felt as numb as her fingers and toes.

"What are you— How did—" She couldn't put words together.

Cash rubbed her arms and hands. "When you didn't show for the meeting with Overstreet, we came looking for you."

Meeting? Images flashed. She was driving. From Atlanta. The box truck.

"They…ran me…off the road." Her teeth chattered, making it hard to speak.

"We saw. Owen called it in while I—" His brows pulled together.

He'd jumped in the water to save her.

She ran her gaze over him. "Your shoulder?"

He couldn't be fully recovered from the injuries he'd suffered in the accident.

Cash waved a hand. "I'm fine."

But from the way he moved, she could tell it must be hurting.

More than gratitude flowed through her. He'd risked his own life for hers.

She rested a hand on his arm and shot him a grateful look.

He shrugged and nodded toward a car parked on the side of the road. Their GBI sedan. Owen stood near it now, phone at his ear. "He's probably checking to see if anyone got a bead on the truck," Cash said.

She hoped they could find the person responsible.

"So, what happened?" he asked.

"I don't know." She reviewed the events in her mind. "I saw the truck right before I got off the freeway, and then they followed me and started ramming into me."

"And you don't know who it was?"

"No idea."

Sirens filled the air. The fire truck and ambulance pulled up, and two paramedics rushed down the hill toward them. She recognized Pete Delaney, who taught CPR classes at the local YMCA. Despite her protests, he loaded her onto a gurney and carried her to the ambulance bay. After checking her vitals and lungs, Pete decided she didn't need to go to the hospital.

"But be sure to go at the first sign of any trouble breathing or other issues," he said.

She promised. He checked Cash as well, coercing him to wear a brace for his shoulder. Then they packed up to leave.

Still damp and cold, she eyed her two rescuers. "Now what?"

"Well," Owen said, both hands on his hips. "We need to get your SUV out of the lake. I've contacted the sheriff's office, and they're sending over their dive team. I've called for a tow truck. And Agent King is on the way. We'll get your vehicle out and take it to the lab to process. See if there's any evidence we can pull to tell us who did this."

"No hits on the BOLO for the box truck?" Cash asked.

Owen shook his head.

So, the person who did this was still out there. She shivered as a breeze blew over her.

Cash looked her way. "We need to change out of these wet clothes."

Owen tossed the keys to the sedan at Cash, who caught them with one hand. "Drive Maya home so she can change. I'll hitch a ride back to the office with King."

She glanced at the lake. "Um…my keys are gone. And my wallet, phone." Everything.

A feeling of despair washed over her. She hadn't felt so lost since her years in the foster system. Moving to a new home with nothing but what she crammed into her backpack. Having no anchor to hold her in one place.

Cash stepped to her side. "We keep extra clothes at the office," he said. "I'll take you there, then we'll work on replacing the rest of your things."

Words failed her. Cash Brenner had come to her rescue, just as she had helped him last night. She hoped this didn't become a pattern. Because now it seemed both of their lives were in danger.

Dry clothes did make a difference. Dressed in an extra uniform, Cash combed his hair back into place and left the locker room of the GBI office. He rapped lightly on the door to the women's quarters.

"Maya? You good?"

The door opened, and she stepped out in his borrowed clothes. She'd showered, and her wavy dark hair hung loose around her shoulders. The sight of her wearing a pair of his track pants and an Atlanta Braves sweatshirt did strange things to him. Maya was a tall woman, but his clothes still hung on her. She looked fragile. Vulnerable.

He wanted to wrap her in a hug and chase away the lost expression she'd worn since the accident.

He cleared his throat. "Will those work?"

"Sure." She rolled up the sleeves of the sweatshirt. "And… thanks." Shifting from one foot to the other, she seemed unsure of her next move.

SAC Overstreet came down the hall carrying a stack of papers. He glanced over the rim of his glasses and took in the two of them. Cash, just released from the hospital, still scratched and bruised from the car wreck, and his left arm in a sling. And Maya, hair still damp and swimming in his borrowed clothes. He wondered if the SAC was about to send them both home.

Unfazed, Overstreet turned toward his office. "Bravo team is assembling in ten minutes. You two should join us."

As he disappeared around the corner, Maya sighed. "Why do I get the idea that wasn't a suggestion?"

Cash had known the SAC long enough to recognize a directive when he heard one. “It wasn’t, but he wouldn’t have invited you without a reason.” He eyed her. She had to be shaken up by the ordeal, but she was trying hard not to show it.

She nodded. “Lead the way.”

They headed to Overstreet’s large office in the corner of building and settled into chairs at the long conference table. He counted the folks gathered in the room. Owen was joined by the rest of their team. Their crime scene specialist, Addie King, and investigative assistant Theodore Watts. Their Assistant Special Agent in Charge, Tommy Hasler. And their computer forensics expert Noah Chandler.

Interesting group. He glanced at Owen, but the man’s face remained passive as he focused on the SAC.

“All right,” Overstreet said. “I want updates on Cash’s case.”

His case? Since when had he become a case? He turned to Owen, but his partner barely gave him a nod before launching into a report.

“Hospital security found the remains of a set of scrubs that had been mostly burned in the incinerator in the basement. We took what was left and sent it to the lab to see if any DNA evidence could be pulled.”

“And?”

“Nothing much, sir. No DNA matches in the system. One partial print, but not enough for a definitive match. We’re running down a couple of possibilities, but it’s too early to say.”

They’d found the scrubs? No one had told him. He resisted the urge to kick Owen under the table and focused on Watts.

“I’ve been working with Chandler on tracking Brenner’s incoming and outgoing calls. Most everything checks out except one call from an unknown number. It was made to his phone at 10:32 p.m. Traces back to a burner phone. No other calls made to any other lines from that number. It’s been offline since that call.”

Noah Chandler spoke up next. "I tracked the number to the cellular carrier and have been working with them on a location for where the phone was purchased. The best we can tell, it was bought near the Raleigh-Durham area yesterday. I'm going through a list of possible purchase sites now, but it's a lot to dig through."

Overstreet nodded. "Pull in more resources if you need them."

"Will do, sir."

The SAC turned to Addie. "Agent King?"

She flicked her eyes toward Cash for a brief second before launching into her report. "Noah pulled the GPS data from Cash's car and phone for me. I've been following his movements for the past few days. He left his house last night shortly after the call at 10:32 p.m. and drove to the industrial park. Of course, since the park covers more than 400 acres, it's not an exact location. We're canvassing various businesses in the area. We've pulled some surveillance footage, but most of the cameras are focused on building security. Not many show the roads around the park. I can see Cash entering by the main road and then leaving. And then when he…crashed. But figuring out where he went inside the park is murkier."

She gave Cash a small smile as if to apologize.

All of this was news to Cash. His team had been investigating him. Without him.

His neck burned hot, but he put a lid on his temper. It wouldn't help if he blew his top at his SAC.

Overstreet sighed and rubbed his eyes. "All right. So, what we've got is a bunch of not much."

"One more thing to add, sir." Owen raised a finger. "I've spoken to the hospital administrator. The syringe used on Cash was full of insulin. Enough to have put Cash into a coma. Or worse." He slid his eyes toward Cash, worry etched on his face. "They've done a detailed inventory, and no medications are missing or unaccounted for. The syringe was brought in by the perpetrator. It didn't originate from the hospital."

"Great," Overstreet said. "So, in addition to not much, we've also got a person with an apparent vendetta against one of our own."

The agents at the table nodded, looks of frustration and concern across their faces.

"It's time to think outside the box." Overstreet motioned to Maya, who hadn't moved since the meeting began. "This is a little unorthodox, but I'm at a loss here. I've got a criminal on the loose, with an active threat against one of my agents. An agent with retrograde amnesia to boot. And a possible citizen in danger, according to today's events. We need answers. And Miss Reid may be the key."

Half a dozen pairs of eyes turned her way. Maya sat up in the chair, although inwardly she wanted to turn and flee down the hallway and out the front door.

Last night, when Special Agent in Charge Overstreet had asked her to come down to the GBI field office, she'd been surprised and intrigued. She wanted to know more about this other case that seemed similar to hers. The Fielding case. But someone was also targeting her and Cash. And an office full of people staring at her was more than she'd bargained for.

Especially with Cash Brenner in the room.

The bruises on his face were still fresh, and the cut above his brow was covered with a bandage. Dressed in his uniform of a black polo shirt and khakis, he matched the rest of the agents around the table.

But Cash always stood out, no matter where he was. Good looks combined with the power of his ice-blue eyes drew attention to him without any effort on his part.

Eyes that were now staring at her intensely.

She pulled her own eyes away and looked up at SAC Overstreet. "I'm not sure what you mean."

Around the table, the expressions of the other agents suggested they were as confused as she was.

"Ladies and gentlemen," Overstreet said. "This is Maya Reid. Some of you already know her. She's a private investigator in the area."

Other than Cash, the only other familiar person in the room was Owen. He smiled and nodded.

Overstreet stepped around the table as he spoke. "Miss Reid is currently investigating a missing person case that bears some important similarities to one of our own cold cases."

He clicked a remote in his hand and a screen on the wall lit up. He began clicking through slides of a presentation. "No doubt most of you will recognize this case."

A few sighs carried across the room when the picture of a young woman showed on the screen. Cash's face dropped, and he rubbed his forehead. Owen laid a hand on Cash's shoulder.

"Elizabeth Fielding," Overstreet said. "Disappeared from the East Ridge University campus four years ago."

The mention of the university caught Maya's attention. She focused on the screen.

"A bright young woman, a good student, who volunteered at the local homeless shelter on weekends." Overstreet clicked the next screen. "Reported missing by her two roommates. When officers searched her room, they found evidence of drug abuse, although both roommates claimed to have no knowledge of Elizabeth ever using drugs. And despite the efforts of the Bureau, the campus police and the county sheriff's office, no leads as to where Elizabeth has gone. She just seemed to vanish."

The details of the case struck her. It was almost as if he were talking about Laurel.

He clicked the last slide and turned the projector off.

"I know this case is a hard one to revisit." Overstreet's gaze landed on Cash. "Agent Brenner has followed a number of leads over the years, but nothing has panned out."

Cash's hands on the table clenched into fists. Maya could tell this case had really gotten to him.

It appeared he had never stopped working on this case, even four years later. Once, on a date, he'd mentioned a lead he had been following that had turned into a dead end. She had seen his passion for solving that case. The look in his eyes when he'd talked about it had made her hurt for him.

She blinked away the image as Owen stood and handed papers around the table. "At the hospital, Maya explained she was looking into the disappearance of Miss Laurel DeWitt. I've put the specs of the case here for you to check out."

Owen sat down, and SAC Overstreet took the lead again. "Since Miss Reid's investigation led her to the industrial park, and Agent Brenner was at the same location for an unknown reason, I believe combining efforts here may bring answers to both mysteries." He nodded to those around the table. "Team, you'll continue to work on Cash's case, as well as returning to the Fielding case. Since no official missing person report has been filed for Miss DeWitt, it's not a GBI investigation. However..." He turned to look at Cash. "Agent Brenner, your assignment will be to shadow Miss Reid as she continues her investigation and help in any way you can. Perhaps the two of you will turn up something that will trigger your memories, as well."

Dread filled her, but words of protest stuck in her throat. She cut her eyes over to Cash, whose face was a mask of stone.

Yes, she could use the help to find Laurel. And she hated to give that up.

But she hated the thought of working with Cash Brenner even more.

Cash stood as the meeting ended and the agents filed out of the office. Maya mumbled a thank-you to SAC Overstreet and exited the room quickly. Cash followed her out into the hall. Her eyes darted toward the front lobby as if she wanted to get out of the building and away from him as soon as possible.

"Everything okay?" he asked.

She took a deep breath and relaxed her stance a fraction. "Sorry. I'm not used to… I felt a little ambushed in that meeting."

"Why?"

One shoulder lifted. "I don't like someone making decisions for me."

He had picked up on her lone wolf tendencies when they dated. Probably one of the reasons she preferred to work as a private investigator. She liked being in control of her own actions.

"You could say no." He hoped she didn't.

Unfolding her arms, she stuck her hands in her pockets. "So…what do we do now?"

"Follow orders."

"I don't work for you." She took a step back.

"That's not what I meant." He cut his eyes toward Overstreet's office. "I have to comply with the SAC's assignment." He turned back to her, his gaze turning soft. "But like it or not, it's to your advantage to have our help."

Both of them had been thrust into this situation without their consent. Now it was up to them to make the best of it.

"What does that look like?" she asked.

"We share info, compare the two cases. Make lists and form an action plan." He motioned for her to follow him down the hall.

"Right now?"

"Why not? You've got something better to do?" His smirk indicated he was teasing her.

"Yeah. I have no car. No purse. No phone." Her face fell. "Not even a key to my house."

It had all been in her vehicle when it went into the lake.

The feeling of panic rushed to his chest again. But she was here. In front of him. Safe and sound.

She looked so lost. Unsure.

What she needed right now was comfort. Not case files.

"I know where there's tea. Organic," he said, remembering her preference for natural things. "How about we grab a cup and then start making a list of what you need?"

Her face relaxed, and she followed him to the break room.

He opened the cabinets until he found the loose-leaf tea one of the agents kept stocked. Eyeing the canister and then the decade-old coffee maker, he stopped. "Um… I'm not sure what to—"

"I've got it." She reached around him and pulled a small, metal orb from the cabinet, then scooped the tea leaves into it.

He watched with fascination as she went through the process of making the tea. Her long, slender fingers danced through each step with the grace of a well-rehearsed ballerina.

She poured the steaming brew into two mugs, added a dollop of honey and handed him one of the cups.

He raised a brow.

"Try it," she urged.

He took a small sip, the taste of cinnamon and cloves mingling with the honey. "Good."

Her lips tugged up in a smile. The first he'd seen since she'd shown up in his life again. He liked what it did to her face. Made him want to brush his fingers along her jawline.

Whoa, Brenner. Don't go there.

Stepping away, he took his mug and settled at the table. "All right, your SUV is being retrieved from the lake. Addie will get it processed at the lab as soon as possible. Owen has made some calls, and a replacement phone is on its way. The DMV is sending over a temporary license."

"They are? Just like that." She sat across from him.

He smiled. "Owen has a way of winning folks over. Once

you contact your insurance company, we can get you a rental to drive. What else?"

She held the mug in her hands, her expression thoughtful. "I should be able to get another set of keys from my landlord. Then I can get my insurance info from my house."

He nodded. "Sounds like a plan. I can drive you over when you're ready."

"Cash, you don't have to—"

He placed a hand on her arm. "Hey, it's fine. I don't mind."

She glanced at his hand. He slid it away.

The impulse to touch her had been instinctual. Like jumping from Owen's car and plunging into the lake after Maya had been. When he'd seen her SUV go over that railing…

He clenched his jaw, remembering the sheer terror he'd felt.

Nothing had mattered. Not Owen's shouts behind him, not the cold of the water, not the pain in his shoulder. Nothing but getting to Maya and pulling her out of the sinking vehicle.

He'd told himself it was his training that had kicked in. Protecting people was what he did.

But there was more to his fear than simply the alarm at seeing a citizen in trouble.

It was Maya. She mattered to him more than he cared to admit. Even after the breakup, he'd thought of her often. He hadn't forgotten her.

She watched him now, the golden flecks in her brown eyes highlighted by the sunlight streaming in from the window.

"Let me check in with Owen." He stood and retreated to his partner's desk.

Retreating was what he did best. Running away from anything that resembled real connection. Or affection. The wall he'd built around his heart had been impenetrable for decades. But Maya Reid seemed to have found the only chink in the fortress. Somehow, she'd made her way inside and burrowed into his heart.

After talking with Owen, he and Maya got into a GBI sedan and headed for Pendleton. "Still live at the same place?"

"Yeah."

Even though they'd dated for three months, he'd only been to Maya's townhouse a couple of times to pick her up for a date. It was another way he kept his distance in relationships. A person's home was a piece of them, a window into their soul.

"So, new question," he said. "What happened with your sister's parents?"

He hadn't pushed her for details at the accident scene, but he needed to know. Now was as good a time as ever.

A frown crossed her face. "They weren't exactly forthcoming."

"What does that mean?"

"Nothing." She turned to look out the window. "Never mind."

He let out a breath. "Maya, you almost died today." His gut clenched even as he said the words. "I'd say the time for keeping things close to the vest is over."

She glanced at him.

"Besides," he said. "I seem to recall you making a promise to the SAC to share information about your case. Our case, now."

"Fine," she said. "You're right, I guess."

He'd count that as a win. "So, catch me up."

They reached the outskirts of Pendleton by the time she'd filled him in on the details of her visit with the DeWitts.

He was surprised at the parents' response to their daughter's disappearance. But she had learned some valuable information, and at least they had a possible lead or two to follow up on.

Cash pulled into Maya's neighborhood of townhomes and parked in the space in front of hers. "Sounds like this Dillon Cordell fellow is our next step. We can start running background on him and then pay him a visit tomorrow."

He opened the door of the sedan.

"What are you doing?" Maya asked.

"We're going to get your insurance information, right?"

"That's not really a two-person job. I can go by myself."

He shut the door and turned to her. "We were shot at last night. I was almost turned into a human pharmacy. You were run off the road today. I think it's best if we assume these are related to our cases—whatever I was working on—and not take any chances." He couldn't believe what he was about to say, but the truth of their situation was too hard to ignore. "There's safety in numbers. So, like it or not, from now on, you're stuck with me."

FIVE

Maya threw her things into her bag with a bit more force than needed the following morning. Unsure of what the day may hold, she packed an extra set of clothes along with the charger for her new phone and some extra cash, since she hadn't been able to replace her credit cards yet.

Yesterday had been a lot to process, from being told she was now working with the GBI, to meeting Laurel's parents, to nearly drowning in Coley Lake.

And then there was Cash. Pulling her from the water, lending her clothes, spending the rest of the afternoon helping her get back on her feet with a new phone, license, rental car and house keys.

Even when he'd gone home for the evening, Cash had made sure a Pendleton City Police cruiser stayed in the parking lot of her townhouse complex all night.

Sleep had come in fits and starts, but every time she'd peeked through her blinds, she'd seen an officer outside. It had brought a level of security she hadn't felt in…well, ever. This helpful and protective side of Cash was new as well. Whether his behavior was motivated by guilt, or he was simply doing his job, a small voice in her head reminded her not to get used to it.

Cash was still Cash. And he would be gone as soon as this case was over.

Her muscles ached from the accident yesterday, but at least

that was the worst of it. She popped a couple turmeric tablets as she downed the last of her ginger tea. With her family history of addiction, she was careful about taking any medications and used natural solutions whenever possible. The fact that her sister now struggled with an addiction hurt to the core.

Cash had sent her a text twenty minutes ago that he was en route. They were going to Dillon Cordell's apartment this morning. Would they find Laurel there?

Her nerves jingled with anticipation.

But she also tried to temper her excitement. She had to be prepared for the condition her sister might be in. If it was true that Laurel wasn't missing but had spent the last few weeks on a binge, she would be in bad shape.

Her new phone buzzed on the counter. Cash was here.

She added protein bars and an extra bottle of water to her bag as the knock sounded on the door. With a quick glance at herself in the mirror, she smoothed a couple stray hairs from her ponytail and opened the door.

Cash's frame filled her doorway. Not dressed in his GBI uniform, he wore a long-sleeved Henley tucked into dark jeans. Freshly showered and shaved, he cut an attractive figure and his look appeared effortless.

She'd changed her outfit three times.

"No uniform?" she asked, trying to distract herself from the way the gray color of his shirt set off the lighter shades of his eyes.

"Thought maybe our guy would be a bit more talkative to two concerned friends of Laurel than law enforcement." He patted his pocket and winked. "But I've got the badge in case he isn't."

"Good idea."

"Ready?" He reached for her bag.

"I've got it."

"Okay." He waited while she locked the door and then led the way to parking lot. "How ya feeling today?"

"Fine."

He raised a brow.

"Sore. But not too bad."

"I know the feeling."

She searched the lot. "Where's your car?"

He motioned toward a silver extended cab pickup. "We're undercover today, remember?"

"Right."

She reached for the door, but he got there before her and opened it.

This already felt too much like a date. Cash standing on her stoop, picking her up in his truck, opening doors for her.

She settled in the seat while he went around and got in.

The smell of his aftershave wafted around the cab.

This was going to be a long day.

Cash filled her in on his research into Dillon Cordell as they drove. According to what he'd uncovered, Dillon lived in an apartment in Dansby, a neighborhood outside East Ridge. The area was known for its low-rent housing and was popular with college students and young professionals. The many bars and clubs also labeled the area as a place for those who liked to party.

"How did my sister, the honor student, get mixed up with someone from Dansby?"

"I pulled his records. Kid's got a rap sheet a few pages thick, too," Cash said.

"What kind of stuff is he into?"

"Mostly petty thefts, disorderly conduct and a couple of minor possession charges. No convictions."

Which made it all the more confusing that her sister would be with him. "I don't get it. What does Laurel see in this guy? Is he rich?"

"Hardly. He's blue-collar. Employer listed as an auto repair shop in town."

None of this made any sense.

She thought back to the pictures she'd seen on Laurel's social media profiles. No boyfriend in any of them. Maya had done her own digging into Dillon Cordell last night, too, but if he had any profiles, she couldn't find them.

They drove through the main strip of Dansby and turned into what appeared to be an industrial area. Old factories and warehouses had been repurposed into loft apartments above shops and restaurants. The whole area gave off a New York City SoHo vibe.

Cash pulled into a parking spot on the street. Maya exited before he could offer to open her door. She needed to set some boundaries in this working arrangement.

She joined Cash on the sidewalk. He checked his phone. "We're looking for 301 River Walk."

"There." Maya pointed to a building painted black with large windows. The sign River Walk Place was painted in gold letters above a glass double door.

"Pretty ritzy for a mechanic," Cash said. He opened the door to a small lobby with a cluster of mailboxes on one wall.

Maya checked the one listed for apartment 301. "No name."

"This was the last-known address listed for him," Cash said. "Let's see if Mr. Cordell is home."

He led the way up the flight of stairs to the upper level.

Sounds of televisions and a thumping beat of music came from various doors as they passed.

They found the apartment with the number 301 in a brass plaque fastened to the door. She took a breath as Cash pressed the small doorbell button on the side.

Her sister could be on the other side of this door.

No one answered.

Cash knocked.

Nothing.

"Let me try," she said. She knocked on the door. "Dillon? It's me."

At Cash's quizzical look, she explained in a quiet voice. "Maybe he'll come to the door if he thinks it's a girl. Seems less intimidating than…" She gestured to him.

He smiled slightly but nodded.

She knocked again. "Laurel?"

"I don't think anyone is home," Cash said. He knocked on the door next to Dillon's. A young woman in a tank top and loose pajama pants opened the door.

"Yes?"

"Hey, I was looking for Dillon. You seen him around?" Cash kept his tone casual and flashed a smile.

Maya felt sorry for the girl. She knew the impact that smile had.

"Uh…no, no. I haven't seen him in…" She thought for a moment. "Probably a couple of weeks. Sorry."

"Okay, thanks."

The door closed with a soft click.

Disappointment flooded her.

She had really hoped to find Laurel, but this felt like another dead end.

Cash read Maya's reaction to not finding Dillon at home. Clearly, she was upset. She kept her eyes down as they left the apartment building and headed back to his truck. He probably should have done a better job at not getting her hopes up.

He clicked the key fob to unlock the doors. Maya hurried to open hers and jumped in. Message received. She didn't want or appreciate him opening the door for her. Too much like a date, he guessed. He didn't blame her. He'd never opened a door for Owen. He needed to remember that, for this case, Maya was his partner. And this was only a temporary work assignment. He climbed into the driver's seat.

"I was really hoping..." She left the thought unsaid.

That she would find her sister.

"It is the middle of the day during the week, after all," he said. "Dillon's probably at work. We'll try there next." He started the truck and backed out of the spot, heading toward the shop listed as Dillon's employer.

Rooster's Auto Repair and Customs was a fifteen-minute drive from downtown Dansby. Not a large building. Or a new one. The place looked a little run-down and could use a good paint job.

How could someone working here afford the loft apartment they'd just seen?

He pulled into the customer parking area. Maya hadn't said anything else on the drive over, and he hadn't felt the need to fill the quiet with small talk, giving her space to process whatever she was feeling.

"You wanna come in with me?" he asked.

She blinked, seeming to notice they had arrived. "Oh. Yeah, of course." She gave him a small smile. "In this together, right?"

"Right."

He'd been the one to say that to her yesterday, but why did those words set off a little alarm in his head?

They walked up to the open garage doors. Three bays were occupied by vehicles in various stages of repair. The sounds of machines mixed with loud rock music from a stereo in the corner.

A man in blue coveralls stopped working on a Dodge Charger and walked over to them. The name tag on his shirt read Bill. "Can I help you?"

"I was looking for Dillon," Cash said, keeping his tone casual. "Is he around?"

Bill sized him up. His eyes flitted to Maya, appreciation showing in his gaze.

Cash took a step closer to her.

"Who's asking?" Bill tore his eyes from Maya.

"Name's Cash. I wrecked my Mustang a couple of weeks ago." He shrugged. "One of my buddies told me Dillon was the best repairman around."

Bill eyed him for a moment, then nodded. "He is. But he's not here."

"Ah, that's too bad. Know when he'll be back?"

"Took the day off."

Cash hadn't anticipated that. But if they had to come back tomorrow, they could.

"Do you know where he might be today?" Maya asked.

Desperation colored her tone. Even Bill seemed to pick up on it.

He narrowed his eyes and surveyed them both again. "Why do you need to know?"

"No reason," Cash answered. "I just really want to get my car back in working order." He wrapped his arm around Maya's shoulders and steered her toward the door. "We can check back tomorrow."

She looked up at him, her eyes imploring.

"Oh, better yet," he said, turning back to Bill, "maybe you could have him call me?"

Bill grabbed a pad of paper from a nearby table and tossed it to Cash. "Sure."

Cash wrote his number down. "Thanks, man."

He ushered Maya out the door before she could say anything else.

"What was that?" she hissed as soon as they reached his truck.

"With a record like he's got, Dillon would take off at the first hint of law enforcement. Sometimes it's good to not go in with guns blazing."

She slammed the door. "And sometimes it is."

"Yeah, but not right now."

"I want my sister back." She closed her eyes.

He squeezed her hand. "I know you do. But we gotta do this right. If Dillon is our only lead, we can't afford to scare him off."

They headed north. No need to stay in Dansby without any clue as to where Dillon could be.

"Can we go to Laurel's apartment?" she asked.

"Sure, but we don't have a search warrant or anything."

"I know, but…" She tucked her bottom lip between her teeth.

"What?"

"I want to talk to Skylar again. I think she may know more than she admitted."

"What makes you think that?"

She shook her head. "I don't know. Just a feeling." Her eyes filled with hope. "Please?"

"It wouldn't hurt. And we've got no other leads to follow today."

He took the road to East Ridge, and Maya directed him to the apartment complex a few blocks from campus. Driving through the university brought back memories of the search for Elizabeth Fielding four years ago.

He understood Maya's desperation. As the days had stretched into weeks with no sign of Elizabeth, her family's despair had grown. And he'd felt much the same.

Was Owen right? Had he been working on Elizabeth's case the night he lost his memory? If so, he prayed he could remember. The young co-ed's face flashed in his mind. And something else. Something…just beyond his grasp. The curtain of his memory closed before he could catch hold of it.

"Cash!"

"What?" He looked up to see the traffic light was red and slammed on his brakes.

He and Maya both jerked forward as their seat belts held them fast.

"Sorry. I was…"

"Did you remember something?"

"I—I don't know. At least, I think I started to, but it went away before I could really get it." He blew out a frustrated breath.

"At least you started to remember. That's a good sign."

"Maybe." He shook his head as if to clear his mind. "How much farther?"

"A block ahead. To the right."

He turned into the complex parking lot and found a spot. He pulled his jacket with the GBI logo on it from his back seat and slipped it on, then pinned his badge to his belt so it could be easily seen.

Maya raised an eyebrow. "I thought it was better to not go in with guns blazing."

"Not this time."

"Why?"

"Skylar's not a flight risk. But if she is hiding something, she'll be more apt to spill it if she knows she's being questioned by the GBI."

Maya tipped her head. "Good thinking."

He smiled. "Not my first rodeo."

They headed to Skylar's building and up the steps to the second floor.

As they waited for Skylar to open the door, he surveyed the parking lot. A dark blue compact drove slowly on the opposite side. Something about it caught his attention.

Had he seen that car before? But where?

Or maybe his mind was playing tricks on him. Being on campus was messing with him.

The door opened. Skylar Hudson was a small-framed brunette with brown eyes that widened when she saw Maya. And then Cash standing behind her.

He unclipped his badge and held it up for her to see. "Skylar

Hudson? Special Agent Cash Brenner with the GBI. I'd like to ask you a few questions about Laurel DeWitt."

Cash wasn't kidding when he'd said he was coming in hot.

Maya sat at Skylar's kitchen table and watched him work. She'd never seen Cash in his official capacity, but he was a wonder to behold. As he questioned Skylar, he walked the line between tough cop and friendly cop like an acrobat on a tightrope.

The way he framed each query left no option but to answer, but his body language, tone of voice and facial expressions evoked a sense of ease and comfort. He wasn't trying to frighten Skylar, but he definitely wanted answers.

He started with questions that Maya already knew the answers to. How long she'd been roommates with Laurel, when was the last time she'd seen Laurel, if she had heard from her since. Skylar's answers were consistent with what she'd told Maya before.

Cash took a sip of the coffee Skylar had offered them, taking his time. He leaned back in his chair slightly. "Had Laurel's behavior changed any over the last few months?"

That was a question Maya hadn't thought to ask.

Skylar's expression showed she was thinking it over. "Yeah, maybe. I mean, more so in the last few weeks before she left."

"How so?" Cash asked.

"Well, she used to be really focused on school. Studied a lot. But then, she started going out more in the evenings, even when she had early classes the next day. Skipped class sometimes. Slept in more."

"When did that start?"

"I guess, maybe, five or six months ago."

"About the time she started seeing Dillon?"

"Yeah."

Cash leaned forward slightly. "And what did you think of Dillon?"

Skylar flipped her hair over her shoulder. "I didn't really know him."

"I find that hard to believe." Cash gestured to the apartment. "I doubt your roommate could be dating someone seriously and never invited him to her apartment or that the two of you never met."

"Well, I mean, I met him. But I didn't know much about him. Laurel…was kinda secretive about her relationship with him."

"That must've been hard for you," he said. "You and Laurel were roommates. Friends. You don't keep secrets from your friends, right?"

"Yeah." Skylar crossed her arms and looked away.

Cash had hit a nerve, Maya could tell.

He cut his eyes towards Maya and nodded his head ever so slightly. He wanted her to jump in.

"Why would she do that?" she asked Skylar.

The young woman shrugged. "I guess because…she knew her family wouldn't approve of him." She looked Maya's way. "He wasn't exactly their kind of people, if you know what I mean."

Having met the DeWitts and then seeing the auto shop where Dillon worked, she knew pretty much what Skylar was getting at.

"How did they meet?" She followed Cash's example and sat back, assuming a relaxed stance.

Skylar glanced from her to Cash and back, seeming to weigh her options. She shrugged a shoulder. "Some party we went to. I don't remember exactly where. One of our sorority sisters invited us, and she drove. It was a house, not too far away, but I wasn't paying attention to how we got there."

That seemed plausible, but Maya felt like there was more Skylar was leaving out.

"So, you remember when they met?" Cash asked.

Skylar nodded. Her expression hardened slightly. "It was

right before the end of fall semester. I remember because we'd been studying hard for final exams, and Laurel said we should go out and blow off a little steam."

"And when did you find out Laurel was dating Dillon?"

"A few weeks later. After we'd come back from Christmas break."

Maybe Laurel hadn't been trying to keep her relationship a secret if they were away for the break. But Skylar seemed so defensive about it.

"You don't like Dillon, do you?" she asked.

Skylar looked down at the table. "Not…not really."

"Any specific reason?" Cash asked.

"He…seemed like bad news." Skylar crossed her arms and looked away again.

The defensive body language made Maya wonder if Skylar was lying, or at least not telling the whole truth. But her expression read worried, upset.

"Do you think Dillon is the reason Laurel started abusing drugs?" Maya asked.

"Probably. I mean, she claimed she hurt her back skiing with her family over the break. But then, she kept taking the pills and got worse and worse." Skylar stood and paced the area between the table and the sofa. "I tried to talk to her about it, you know. But she would brush me off and say everything was fine. And then she'd get mad whenever I would ask about the pills or Dillon or anything."

"I know it's hard to watch someone you care about go through something like this," Cash said.

Skylar nodded, swiping tears from her cheeks.

Maya swallowed around the lump in her throat. Images of her mother's descent into addiction crossed her mind. To think her sister had gone down the same path broke her heart.

Cash walked to Skylar and laid a hand on her shoulder. "We

need to find your friend. Laurel could be in real trouble. Is there anything else you can tell us that might help?"

"I don't know."

"How about somewhere we might find Dillon?" Maya said, stepping over to them. "He wasn't at home or at work."

Skylar seemed to waver, then sighed. "He hangs out at a club called Aces most evenings. You could probably find him there."

Aces. Maya had seen the sign when they were driving through Dansby.

"That's great, Skylar," Cash said, giving her an appreciative look.

"Yes," Maya said. "Thanks for your help." A sliver of hope ran through her. Finally, something they could work with.

She glanced at Cash, and he nodded. Time to go. They exited the apartment.

"I hope you find her," Skylar said from the doorway. "Because she's left me here to pay all the bills by myself. And I don't have rich parents to help me out."

The thread of anger in her voice surprised Maya, but Cash nodded, waved goodbye and led them down the stairs.

"What was that?" Maya asked when they reached the truck.

Cash shrugged. "I mean, I guess I can see her point. She is stuck with the full load now. And sometimes it's easier to be angry than hurt or worried."

She had to agree. In the foster homes, anger had been her best friend and one of the only ways she coped with losing her mother and then her baby sister.

"So, do we go to Aces now?" She buckled her seat belt as Cash started the vehicle.

"Not yet." He tapped his phone. "Their website says they don't open until seven. We've still got a few hours."

"Okay, so now what?"

"Let's head back to the office. I need to check on a couple

of things." His brow furrowed as he glanced in the rearview mirror.

"What is it?" She turned to look behind them, but nothing seemed amiss. Only the apartment parking lot with a few cars scattered about.

Cash shook his head and then put the truck in gear. "It's nothing."

It wasn't necessarily nothing. At least, he couldn't be sure. But how could he explain to Maya that his missing memories felt like being caught in a carnival house of mirrors? Like his eyes were telling him things his mind couldn't verify.

He kept watch for the blue hatchback, but it hadn't followed them when they'd left Skylar's apartment complex.

Shaking off the feelings, he concentrated on the road and the plan forming in his mind. They needed to find Dillon Cordell. Hopefully, he would show up at Aces tonight. But they would need a special approach to get him to talk. And he would need both Owen and Addie's help.

"So, catch me up on the Elizabeth Fielding case." Maya's words brought him back to the present. The usual tension he felt along his neck and shoulders arose whenever the subject of the Fielding case came up. He didn't like talking about the investigation he counted as his biggest failure. But since the SAC thought Laurel's case might be connected, it wouldn't hurt to discuss it with Maya. She might see something that he'd missed before. "What would you like to know?"

"Any new developments in the last two years?"

"No." He sighed.

"Okay, let's go back to the beginning. How did you get involved at first? I know the GBI doesn't investigate every person that goes missing in Georgia."

"Right. We're called in by request of local agencies, usually. Sometimes the governor will get involved, put us on high-profile cases."

"Is that what happened?"

"It was both, actually. East Ridge University has their own police department. With a campus that large and a student body in the thousands, they have an ample and very effective agency. But with this case being a missing student and the leads running cold, they asked us to step in. About the same time the governor called Director Higgins to pull us in. The case was making national headlines, and he wanted to show they were making every effort possible."

"I remember when it happened. Seemed like every agency in Georgia was looking for her."

And yet, they'd all come up empty. His hands fisted around the steering wheel.

Maya continued. "I volunteered with the search teams a few times. When they were canvassing the woods near campus and needed extra boots on the ground."

"You told me about that."

"I figured my training might help." She looked his way. "I'm sorry we couldn't find her."

So was he.

"How did you get stuck with being with lead investigator?"

He shrugged. "I didn't get stuck. I volunteered."

Overstreet hadn't been too keen on the idea, but Cash had persisted until he'd gotten the job. Still new to the team, Cash had felt the need to prove himself. And his ego had led him to believe he could succeed.

How arrogant he'd been.

He prayed his pride hadn't caused him to miss important information that could've led to Elizabeth's whereabouts.

"Why in the world would you want a case like that?"

"She… Elizabeth…reminded me of my sister."

"She did? I don't think you ever told me that."

Another thing he'd never shared with her. In the months they had dated, he'd kept the details of his dysfunctional family history to himself.

"Yeah, Katie's three years younger than me. A little older than Elizabeth was at the time, but still, I couldn't help but think of Katie. Same hair color, same build. Both talented musicians."

The similarities hadn't stopped there. The more he'd learned about Elizabeth, the more he'd connected her to his sister.

A dangerous mistake for any law enforcement officer to make. Getting too close to a case, becoming too personally involved.

So many things he'd do differently if given the opportunity. The Fielding case was one regret.

Maya was another.

"It bothers you, doesn't it?"

She meant the case. Not their relationship.

He glanced her way. Her dark eyes searched him. He nodded. No need to hide it. Everyone knew this was the case he couldn't let go.

"Why?" she asked.

He could name off the reasons, but there was only one that mattered. "I failed."

Warm pressure met his arm as she rested a hand on him. "I'm sorry."

He pushed the emotions aside.

How was he talking to her about this? These were feelings he'd only shared once with Owen, when the struggle was still fresh.

What was it about Maya that made him want to open up?

He glanced her way. Her expression held no judgment. No, instead he saw understanding. A mutual feeling of regret at having let someone down. Of losing someone important.

Longing and fear sliced through him.

He had to help Maya find her sister. He couldn't have another failure on his conscience. But it was more than that.

He couldn't let Maya down.

Not again.

"Are you sure this is the best idea?" Owen shut his locker door and turned to Cash.

"What's wrong with my plan?" Cash leaned against the vanity. He'd explained the strategy to Owen and Addie once he and Maya had returned to the GBI office. They were going undercover. Posing as couples. Owen and Addie would go with Cash and Maya to the club in Dansby, where they hoped to find Dillon Cordell.

According to the patrols posted outside Dillon's home and work, he hadn't returned to either location. Unable to find him otherwise, the club was their next best chance. And based on his rap sheet, Dillon would likely clam up in an interrogation room and call for his lawyer. Cash's idea was to have Addie and Maya approach Dillon at the club and gain intel on where Laurel might be. With no missing person report officially filed for Laurel, they didn't have enough to bring Dillon in for questioning. The covert operation was their best chance at seeing if he were truly involved in her disappearance.

Owen adjusted the collar of his shirt and ran a comb through his hair. He'd changed out of his uniform into street clothes in preparation for tonight's mission. "Nothing's wrong with the plan itself."

"Okay, then what's the problem?"

Owen rested both hands on his hips and surveyed Cash. Why did Cash feel the need to squirm under his partner's assessment?

"If you're worried about taking Maya," Cash said, "she can handle herself. Private eye, remember? She's done undercover work before. And I think she's safer with us than without us."

He couldn't forget that someone had run her car off the road and into the lake.

"I agree. And I'm not worried about Maya. I know she's capable." He speared Cash with his gaze. "How are you dealing with everything?"

"Me? I'm fine. Back to normal." He moved his shoulder to prove it.

It wasn't all true, though. His memory of where he'd been before the accident remained lost in his subconscious. But that shouldn't hinder his ability to find and question a suspect.

Owen had never doubted Cash before. Where was this coming from?

"I'm not talking about physically." Owen took a seat on the bench between the rows of lockers. He motioned for Cash to do the same. "I mean…how are you doing? You've been attacked. So has Maya. We've got no leads on either the box truck or the mystery nurse. Has any part of your memory from that night returned?"

Cash ground his teeth. "Not yet." As much as he'd tried to force it, his memory remained blank.

"Okay. And working with Maya? Given your history…this can't be easy. For either of you."

Cash settled on the bench and met Owen's gaze. "We're doing fine."

Owen tilted his head.

"Okay, okay," Cash said. "There's been a little awkwardness, but nothing that would keep us from doing our jobs. We're both invested in finding her sister and figuring out who's after us."

"I saw the way you went after her in the lake."

He was right, and Cash couldn't deny it.

It all washed over him again. The feeling of helplessness when he realized her car was going over the bridge. The rush to get to her. The panic when he'd seen the water flooding into her vehicle.

And the thought that he might lose Maya forever.

He tried shrugging it off. "I was just doing my job, man. You know that."

Owen shook his head. "That wasn't a normal, impulsive Cash level reaction. The look on your face. That was sheer terror."

Cash crossed his arms, his defenses rising. "Fine. I didn't want her to die. Does that make me a terrible person?"

"No. It just means you care about her. A lot."

"Okay, now you're talking nonsense." Cash stood and walked away.

Caring about someone meant being vulnerable. Open. Honest.

And it only led to hurt.

To pain. Like his mother had gone through every time his dad had left. Always wondering if he'd come back. And dreading the moment he would leave again.

No, he wouldn't put himself or anyone else through that.

Especially someone like Maya. Someone brave and honest. Caring. She deserved much better than him.

Owen clapped a hand on his shoulder. "Sorry, man. I didn't mean to—"

"No, it's fine." He turned to face his partner. "No problem."

"I only meant to say that this setup tonight, pretending to be on a date, as a couple…it could send some mixed signals. Be careful."

"Yeah, I get you." He nodded. "And I will. Be careful, that is."

Owen left, and Cash stood in the empty room, gathering his thoughts.

Yes, he had to be careful tonight. Not only was Maya's life in his hands. But her heart might be as well.

And that was the most dangerous threat of all.

Maya stared out the window of Cash's truck, watching the buildings slide by as they drove into Dansby. She'd been deposited into the back seat with Special Agent Addie King, who had spent the last half hour of travel chattering about the ups and downs of training her new puppy.

Not that Addie was annoying. She was sweet and kind with a good sense of humor. Under other circumstances, Maya would have liked to get to know the agent better. She had a feeling they could become good friends.

But her nerves jangled too much to keep up her end of the conversation. Addie seemed to have taken her silence as a void that needed to be filled with stories of Buttercup, the golden retriever.

Or maybe she was trying to take Maya's mind off what lay ahead.

Maya wasn't nervous about going undercover. Or confronting Dillon Cordell. She was more than ready to grab the slug by the shirt collar and demand to know where her sister was.

Every moment they spent looking for Dillon meant more time that Laurel was missing.

Even if she didn't find Laurel tonight, she hoped they could get at least one step closer. Dillon was the last person to have contact with her sister. If he wasn't involved, maybe he could point them in the right direction.

Someone seemed intent on keeping them from finding her. Given Laurel's addiction issue, she could have gotten mixed up with some very bad people. What had her little sister gotten herself into?

"All right," Cash said from the driver's seat. "We should be at Aces in about ten minutes. Everyone clear on the plan?"

Both Owen in the front passenger seat and Addie beside her voiced their agreement. Maya added her yes.

And that was the other reason her palms were sweaty and her pulse was racing. Tonight, she was posing as Cash's date.

Once inside the club, Cash and Owen would hang back while

Addie and Maya were to approach Dillon and pretend to be friends of Laurel, casually asking if he'd seen her lately.

It was a good plan. Maya couldn't argue with that. Dillon might be more responsive in that environment, and she hoped they could get him talking.

But pulling off the part of Cash's date would be much trickier. She'd been Cash's date before, and the memories sent butterflies dancing through her stomach. Cash on a date was a much more charming and attentive version of himself than Cash on a case.

She needed to remember tonight was not real. She had been on the receiving end of that charm before, and the aftermath was a valley of hurt she'd rather not visit again.

Cash pulled into a parking spot on the street about a block from the club. They got out, and the beat from the music pouring out of the building thumped into her chest. Club patrons were spilling onto the sidewalk, the sounds of laughter surrounding them.

Owen waited for Addie to join him, and he casually dropped an arm over her shoulders as they slipped easily into their undercover roles. If she didn't know better, she would think they were a real couple.

Could she and Cash pull off the same facade?

He stepped to her, pocketing his keys, and held out his hand. Wariness flitted across his eyes as he waited for her to take it.

With a quick breath, she grasped his hand. Ignoring the electricity that traveled up her arm, she pasted on a smile as they strode into the club.

Lights and sounds assaulted her senses. The club was packed with young people dancing and milling about in groups. Cash held tight to her hand as he navigated their way through people to reach the main room.

Owen found an empty table, and they settled in. Maya scanned the crowd, looking for someone who matched the picture of Dillon from his rap sheet. So far, she didn't see anyone that fit. She wanted to panic. What if he didn't show tonight?

Cash leaned close, draping an arm around her. "Don't worry. It's still early. He'll show tonight, I know it."

Shivers traveled down her spine as his warm breath tickled her ear. The smell of his aftershave filled her nose.

Keeping up the charade, she giggled as if he'd said something funny, and he flashed a thousand-watt smile, sending her stomach to her toes.

Careful. She reminded herself to concentrate on finding Dillon.

She sipped the club soda Cash ordered for her and let her gaze travel the crowd without appearing like she was searching.

A slow song came on. Owen nodded at Cash, and then he and Addie walked to the dance floor.

Cash slipped his hand into hers. Oh no. He wasn't about to suggest that they—

"May I have this dance?" His voice and his eyes were soft. Alluring.

Everything in her screamed no.

His brows dipped. Her hesitation bothered him.

He leaned in again. "We need to spread out. Owen and Addie will take the left side of the room. We'll take the right."

And slow dancing would give them an excuse to check out the crowd.

Her heartbeat slowed a fraction. Undercover. *We're undercover.* She repeated the mantra as she nodded, and Cash led her to the dance floor.

He slipped an arm around her waist, holding her hand in his other, and pulled her closer.

Mercy, it felt good to be held in his arms.

She told herself not to enjoy it.

"Relax," Cash whispered into her ear. "We're supposed to be having fun, remember?"

Easy for him to say.

"See anything?"

She scanned the room. "Not yet."

Maya tamped down her anxiety. If Dillon didn't show up tonight…

She couldn't go there. They needed to find him. Needed answers.

Laurel's life might depend on it.

Cash pressed his cheek against hers, scattering her thoughts again.

Man, he was a good actor.

Had he only been acting with her two years ago? He'd seemed so sincere. And things had been going so well with them. Until—

Out of the corner of her eye, she saw movement at the bar and stiffened.

"You see him?" Cash asked.

She nodded. Dillon. She was positive.

"Alone?"

"Yeah."

"Good. I'll text Addie, and you two converge. Strike up a conversation, but keep it light—"

"I know what to do, Cash."

"Right. Sorry."

He released his hold on her and pulled out his phone. She smoothed a hand down her hair. She'd worn it loose and wavy tonight.

As relieved as she was that Dillon had shown up tonight, Maya struggled with anger and resentment. How could he be here, having a good time, when her sister was missing? Didn't he care? Or did he have something to do with it? Only one way to find out.

Getting a nod from Cash that Addie was on her way, Maya walked to the bar. Energy coursed through her, but she forced herself to slow down, smile, act like every other patron in the club.

She reached the bar and stepped in close to her target. “Can I get a club soda?” she said when the bartender turned her way.

“Oh, excuse me.” She purposefully bumped into Dillon’s arm. He turned, and she stared into the eyes of the man who held her sister’s fate in his hands.

SIX

Dillon Cordell had movie-star good looks. Jet-black hair and deep brown eyes. A chiseled jaw with a dimple in his chin.

Maya could see why her sister would be attracted to him.

"Sorry," she said as she sat down next to him. "It's crowded in here."

"Don't worry about it." Dillon smiled, charm oozing from every pore.

"You're…uh, Darren, right?" She feigned forgetting his name.

"Dillon," he corrected.

"Oh, right. Dillon. Sorry."

"No problem." He checked her out, and Maya fought the urge to cringe. "Do we…know each other?"

"Yeah," she said. "I mean, we've met before."

"That seems unlikely. I would've remembered you." He edged closer. "What's your name again?"

"Marley." She used the code name they'd settled on earlier.

"Well, it's nice to officially meet you, Marley."

This guy was slick. Too smooth. Maya's creep meter went off the charts.

Addie approached, and Maya waved her over, using the agent's code name. "Addison!"

Owen and Cash hung back. Far enough not to alert Dillon, but close enough they could intervene if needed.

"Hey, girl!" Addie gave her a quick hug. "Good to see you."

"You, too. Say, you remember Dillon, right?" She gestured to him.

He perked up as Addie gave him the once-over. "Yeah, I think so," she said. "Weren't you at that party last week?"

"Nope, wasn't me."

"Oh. Must have been someone else."

"Well, if you two ladies were there, I'm sure sorry I missed it."

Addie giggled, keeping up the act.

Maya snapped her fingers. "No, I've got it. I know where I've seen you. You're dating Laurel, right? Laurel DeWitt?"

His eyes widened for a second. He glanced between the two of them. "You...you know Laurel?"

"Yeah," Addie said. "She lives in my apartment building." She frowned. "But I haven't seen her in a few weeks. Wonder where she's been?"

Maya shrugged. "I don't know. I haven't seen her in a while, either." She turned to Dillon. "Do you know where's she been?"

He looked away. "No, I... I don't." He stood, starting to leave.

"Are you still seeing her?" Addie pressed a hand to his arm and gave him a coy smile.

Dillon looked from her to Maya. "Actually, we, uh...broke up. A couple of months ago."

"Really? I had no idea."

That had to be a lie. Skylar hadn't said anything about them breaking up. And Dillon was a bit too eager to escape their company. He obviously wasn't telling them the truth.

"That's too bad," Maya said. "You know, I'm pretty sure I still have her jacket I borrowed. I need to get it back to her." She looked Dillon in the eye. "You're sure you don't know where she is?"

Addie propped her arm on Maya's shoulder, and Maya got the message. Back off. She was pressing Dillon a little too hard.

But she was so close. She needed to know where Laurel was, and this creep had to know something. He just wasn't willing to tell.

Dillon narrowed his eyes, then stood, leaning into Maya's space. "What's your deal? Who are you really?"

"Hey, babe." Owen showed up at Addie's elbow, Cash right behind him. "Everything okay here?"

Dillon backed up a step. "What is this? You two a couple of cops or something?"

Owen chuckled. "Only wondering what was taking my girl so long with my drink." He draped his arm around Addie.

Cash didn't say anything, but Maya could feel his presence behind her.

Addie spoke up. "Sorry, babe. We were talking about our friend Laurel."

Desperation filled her. Maya touched Dillon's arm, and she tried to keep her voice casual. "Are you sure you don't know where she is? I'm worried about her, that's all."

Dillon let out a huff. "All right, look, I don't know what's going on here, or who you people are. But I'm telling you. I don't know where she is. She's a druggie, okay?" He wiped a hand down his face. "The chick's been strung out for a while now, and I got tired of it, you know? I told her if she didn't stop, we were through. So, she took off. No idea where." He backed away. "Leave me alone."

Maya felt like she'd been struck, hearing Dillon talk about her sister like that.

Dillon blended into the crowd, and she lost sight of him. She wanted to go after him, grab him by the shoulders, and make him tell her where Laurel was.

As if reading her thoughts, Cash pressed a hand on her shoulder to keep her in place. "Let him go. He's not going to talk."

"But he knows something. I know he does." She turned to face him, frustration burning inside her.

"Of course he does. But we can't push it."

"So, what? You're giving up?"

"Nope." Cash's eyes were hard as steel. "Not at all. Now, we go to plan B."

"Which is?"

He nodded. "We watch Dillon tonight, and when he leaves, we follow."

Cash drummed his thumbs on the steering wheel of his truck, keeping beat along with the song on the radio. Beside him, Maya sat silently, staring out the window of the passenger seat.

She was done taking a back seat in the search for her sister. Both figuratively and literally, as she'd insisted on sitting in the front during the stakeout.

They'd been posted outside Aces for a couple of hours now, waiting for Dillon to leave. Cash had moved his truck to a spot with full view of the front of the building without being obvious.

Owen and Addie had stayed in the club to keep an eye on him.

A commercial came on the station, and Cash flipped the radio off.

Maya hadn't said anything for a while. He could tell something was bothering her, and it wasn't only Dillon's claim that he didn't know Laurel's whereabouts.

"You did good in there," he said, hoping to coax a response from her.

She shrugged. "Not good enough."

"Hey." He rested his hand on top of hers. "It wasn't your fault. Dillon was never going to admit anything that could incriminate him. He's been around the block too many times, knows the drill. The kid is a lowlife, but he's not stupid."

Maya pulled her hand from under his. He didn't want to admit how much he missed the contact. She was so close he could smell the soft vanilla scent of her shampoo. But he was dangerously near crossing the line with her. Tonight had reminded him of how it had been when they were dating. Holding her in his arms while they were dancing…it had affected him more than he let on. It had taken a tremendous amount of self-control to let go of her when she'd spotted Dillon. He'd wanted to hold her a while longer.

"That's not it," she said.

"What?" He'd lost the thread of the conversation.

She'd pulled her long waves back into the ponytail, a sure sign she was stressed.

"I mean, yeah, I'm frustrated that he didn't tell us anything. But that's not what…" She let out a breath.

"It's what he said about Laurel, isn't it? About her addiction?"

She nodded. In the light from the streetlamps outside, he could see a lone tear track down her cheek.

He gripped the steering wheel to keep from brushing it away.

She swiped at it. "Our mom had an addiction, too. It's what drove my dad away." She shifted in the seat, turning to face him. "He was trying to get custody of us, but he was killed in a car accident. That pushed my mom over the edge, and she disappeared into her addiction. About a year later, she overdosed."

His chest tightened at the hurt lacing her words. "Is that when you and Laurel went into foster care?"

"Yeah. About six months later, Laurel was adopted."

He heard the words she left unspoken. "And you weren't."

His heart broke for her. He knew firsthand what it was like to have your world crumble. To have your security pulled out from under you. But he'd always had his mom and siblings, even when his dad was MIA. He'd never felt the level of alone that Maya had felt.

She shrugged. "I was older. Laurel was only a year old. Most people want to adopt a baby, not a nine-year-old. Especially not one labeled as a troublemaker."

"What? You? I can't imagine that." His attempt to lighten the moment coaxed a smile out of her.

"Yeah, well, sometimes you just gotta fight."

Another thing they had in common. He had learned to deal with his hurt and anger by lashing out at anyone who crossed him.

"Sometimes, you do."

She looked his way, and he shrugged. "I was quite the little scrapper back in the day."

"I can't imagine." She echoed his words, a smile on her lips.

He chuckled. They both needed the moment of levity. But she needed something else. Reaching for her hand again, he squeezed. "And sometimes you need to let God fight your battles." A lesson he was still learning. Trusting someone to fight for him and not against him was a foreign concept.

Her eyes turned serious. "You think He's fighting for my sister?"

"I do."

"Are we going to find her?" Her question came out in a whisper, a desperate plea.

He wanted to assure Maya that they were going to find Laurel, that he would fight for her. But that wasn't a promise he could make.

Not to her.

Not to anyone.

His failure at finding Elizabeth Fielding was a stark reminder.

The back doors opened, and Addie and Owen piled in. The moment was broken. Maya retreated to her side of the truck.

"He's on the move," Owen said.

Cash spied Dillon leaving the club and heading toward his car. After running the plates of the vehicles parked in front of Aces, they'd picked out Dillon's bright orange Camaro. The kid wasn't going for subtlety in his choice of rides, that was for sure. Loud and flashy. It reminded Cash of a male peacock strutting his feathers to attract the females.

"Who is he with?" Maya asked.

Cash peered through the darkness. Dillon had someone with him. "A female, blonde hair, red dress."

"I didn't notice him with a date earlier," Addie said.

"I don't think he came with one." Owen peered through a small pair of binoculars. "But he's definitely leaving with one."

"And maybe not of her own free will." The woman with Dillon stumbled down the sidewalk, and he all but carried her to the car. She was either drunk or drugged.

Maya turned to him. "Should we do something?"

"It's not against the law to give someone a ride," he said. "We can't arrest him."

"But…" Maya looked at the couple and then back to him, disbelief showing on her features. "She could be in trouble."

Everything in him screamed to go in for the rescue, but he shook his head. "If we grab him now, he'll have us for false arrest or plead out, and then he'll be gone. We need to let this play out, follow him, and see where he goes."

"He could lead us to Laurel." Addie reached from the back seat and squeezed Maya's arm.

Maya huffed and slumped into the seat, but she conceded with a nod.

Cash put the truck in gear and slowly pulled onto the street as Dillon's car headed out and around the curve. Keeping a safe distance so as to not alert Dillon that he was being followed, Cash navigated the streets a few car lengths behind the Camaro. At least the bright color of the car made it easy for him to keep it in sight.

After a couple of miles, Dillon made a series of turns, then sped up.

"He's on to us," Owen said.

"Maybe not," Cash said. The traffic was lighter on this side of town. Perhaps Dillon felt he could drive faster.

But the Camaro was rapidly leaving them behind.

Cash sped up, but a sudden shutter ripped through the truck.

"What was that?" Maya asked.

A loud pop sounded from under the vehicle, and the steering wheel seemed to lock up.

"I—I don't know. Something's wrong. I've got no power steering." He pressed the brakes to try to pull over, but the pedal went all the way to the floor. "And no brakes!"

"Cash?" Maya's voice went up an octave.

With no brakes and no steering, the truck continued down the road. A car coming from the other direction veered out of the way and honked the horn as Cash's truck went over the yellow line.

He had to stop the vehicle before they crashed into something or someone. "Hold on, everyone!"

Spying an empty parking lot, he wrangled the steering wheel with all he had to aim the truck into the lot. His shoulder screamed in protest, and he wasn't sure he could get the truck turned in time.

Hands slipped between his. Maya leaned over, pulling on the wheel herself.

Together, they got the truck aimed in the right direction. They missed the drive, and the truck bounced over the curb and took out a small sign.

But they landed in the lot.

He slowly began shifting the truck into a lower gear and began gently pressing on the emergency brake. His defensive driving training had taught him that doing either too fast would cause the vehicle to spin out of control.

Finally, the truck slowed and then rolled to a stop at the other end of the parking lot, brushing up against a clump of hedges.

He shifted into Park and pressed the emergency brake fully, then turned the ignition off.

Taking a breath, he turned to check out his passengers. "Everyone okay?"

"Yeah, we're good—" Owen's words died as a shot rang out.

"Get down!"

Maya ducked into the seat at Cash's command. The window behind her shattered, spraying glass over her back.

"Shots fired, shots fired!" Addie yelled into her phone, giving their location to the dispatcher on the other end.

"Where are they?" Cash had his gun drawn.

"Northeast, I think," Owen responded.

"Dispatch says Dansby PD are two minutes out."

A lot could happen in two minutes. Cash's truck wasn't operational. They couldn't make a getaway.

Another shot shattered the back window.

They were sitting ducks in the truck.

"We can take cover behind the bushes," Cash said.

"And then what?" Maya wasn't sure at all about his plan.

"One step at a time." He motioned to Owen and Addie. "Shots are coming from the passenger side. You two cover us. We'll slip out my side, and then we'll cover you."

"Roger that." Owen pivoted so he could shoot out the back window.

Cash opened his door and got out, then motioned to Maya. "Crawl over the seat to my side. Stay low."

She hesitated, weighing her options. Another shot, and the agents returned fire.

"Come on, Maya." Cash held out a hand. "Trust me."

Did she? Emotions warred with logic. She couldn't stay in the truck. Cash's way was the only choice.

She shimmied over the seats, grasping his hand as she

crawled out of the truck. As soon as her feet were on the ground, Cash was pushing her ahead of him. “Behind the bushes. Go!”

They reached the cover of the hedges, and Maya dropped to the ground. Heart pounding in her ears, ice running through her limbs.

Cash knelt beside her. “You good?”

She had expected a bullet in the back, but they’d made it to safety. “Yeah.”

“Help me cover them?”

Pulling her firearm, she found a low spot in the bushes. “Ready.”

“Owen,” Cash called, getting himself in position. “We got you.”

Maya and Cash began firing as Owen and Addie got out of the truck and ran toward them.

Addie stumbled, and Owen grabbed her, pulling her behind the bushes.

“She’s hit!” he called.

Maya went to her.

Addie held her left arm. “Just a graze.”

The gunfire stopped.

“Shooter’s on the run,” Cash said.

“Go after him,” Addie said. “I’m good.”

He and Owen exchanged a look, and Cash glanced at Maya.

“I’ve got it, Cash.” She motioned him away. “Go get the guy.”

With a nod, he stood, and the two men took off.

Fear slid through her veins, but she focused on Addie. “How bad is it?”

“Stings, but it’s okay. It really was just a graze.” The agent pressed a hand on her wound.

“Dansby PD will be here any minute.” The statement was to reassure herself as much as Addie. She was scared for them, but even more scared for Cash and Owen, chasing the unknown shooter through the dark.

Sirens sounded in the distance. Help was coming.

A rustling sound brought both of their firearms up.

"It's us." Cash sounded out of breath.

The two agents came into view. Owen held his side as Cash bent over, resting his hands on his knees.

"And?" Maya asked.

"Shooter got away."

Her gut clenched and tears sprung to her eyes.

Cash sat on the ground next to her as the sirens came closer. "Hey, it's okay. We're all right now."

Shaking her head, she turned to him. "No, we're not." Tears welled in her eyes, followed by anger. "We lost Dillon. How will we find Laurel now?"

Cash crawled from under the truck and clicked off his flashlight. He'd checked the motor and then the wires and hoses. Then, he'd gone underneath and checked out the damage. The cause of the near-crash was clear.

"How's it look?" Owen asked.

"Someone cut the brake line and the power steering hose. Not all the way through, but enough that it would leak out." And it was a professional job, too. If he weren't so familiar with automobiles, he might have missed the cuts.

"Any idea who?"

"Only someone like a mechanic, someone like Dillon Cordell, would know exactly how to cut to cause the problem without it being noticeable. But when did he have time to do that?" He had arrived at the club after them, but once they'd questioned him, he had stayed inside the club until they'd seen him leave.

"Dillon had no way of knowing we were coming to question him."

Owen was right. Dillon had seemed genuinely surprised when Cash and Owen had joined Maya and Addie. And when the questions had turned to Laurel's whereabouts.

The tow truck driver pulled into the lot and got out. Cash nodded for him to go ahead and load his truck onto the trailer. "This needs to go to the GBI lab in Gadden Valley," he told the man. He wasn't sure if it was salvable. Most of the windows were broken and bullet holes riddled the side.

Addie had been checked and released by the paramedics. She would head the team searching the truck for any evidence of who might have done this.

"Addie and I can hitch a ride with the tow truck," Owen said. "You and Maya can ride back with Overstreet."

The SAC had arrived in his sedan a few minutes ago.

"I'd rather go back to Aces for a bit," Cash said. "See if Watts and Chandler have got a positive ID."

Overstreet had sent the other two agents of Bravo team to the club to see if anyone there knew the young woman who'd left with Dillon. Cash also wanted to go through the security footage to see if they could get a clear picture of her.

Owen tipped his head toward the SAC's car. "You taking her with you?"

Maya sat in the front passenger seat, head leaned onto the headrest, eyes closed.

She was mad.

Not at Cash. It wasn't his fault the truck had malfunctioned. Or that they'd been shot at.

But they'd lost Dillon. And his passenger. And another opportunity to find Laurel.

"As if I have a choice," he murmured. No way would Maya agree to sit this one out. Not while there was potentially another missing woman.

Dansby City Police Department had taken over the scene. Cash had given them a description of Dillon's car and tag number. He'd let them know Dillon may have a passenger who could be drugged and in possible danger.

It was the best he could do for now.

But it wasn't enough.

He couldn't be sure of the state the young woman was in, or if she had left with Dillon of her own accord. If Dillon hurt her…

He slammed a fist into his palm.

Maya was right. They should've intervened. The girl's safety should have come first.

Owen climbed into the tow truck's cab with Addie, and they headed out.

Cash walked to the sedan, rubbing his aching shoulder. He needed aspirin, but that would have to wait.

"Watts called. They're ready for you." SAC Overstreet stood near the sedan. He eyed Cash. "You good?"

"Fine. Just a little sore." No way would he admit to the level of pain shooting through him. "Did they get an ID on the girl?"

"A couple of possibilities, I think. They need you and Miss Reid to take a look."

"Okay, let's go." Cash climbed into the back seat. He was down two vehicles now and would need to either borrow a car or rent one. "Anything from Dansby PD on the shooter?"

"Negative, but they are still patrolling the area."

The ride back to the club was a quiet one. Overstreet wasn't one for idle chatter, and Cash didn't feel like talking. Maya had stayed silent since her remark about losing Laurel.

Addie had tried comforting her, but Maya had retreated into her own misery.

And Cash was the last person who should try to coax her out of it. He sat solidly in his own boiling pot of pain, anger and regret. No memories had returned.

All he could do now was concentrate on this case and pray something would loosen the clog in his brain.

Overstreet pulled up to Aces, and they all entered the club again. This time, he and Overstreet showed their badges. No need to be undercover now.

The manager led them to the back office, where Watts and

Chandler watched a monitor with the night's footage. The room was small, and with all five of them crowded in, it felt even smaller.

"Catch us up," Overstreet said.

"Okay," Watts said. "We used your description of the young woman and what she was wearing. Some of the patrons said they knew her. We got three names. Chandler's running them now to check for licenses."

Noah Chandler nodded as he scrolled through his own laptop. "I'll let you know as soon as I get them."

Watts continued. "In the meantime, I've been going through the footage since the club opened. You two take a look and let me know if you see her."

Cash and Maya maneuvered until they were in front of the monitor, and Cash clicked to start the recording. A couple of women matching their description entered at various times.

He turned to Maya. "I see a couple of possibilities. You?"

She shook her head. "We were too far away to get a good look, but she was blonde and wearing a red dress. It could be her or her. Or even her." She pointed to a couple of the women on the screen.

"Agreed. We'll have to forward the footage and see if we can spot her talking to Dillon." He clicked a button to speed up the recording. "Okay, there we are."

On the screen, he and Maya came in the front door behind Owen and Addie.

How natural they looked, holding hands, sitting together at the table. Maya pretending to laugh at him.

Then, they'd stood and walked to the dance floor. His neck heated as he watched himself pull her to him, holding her close as they swayed to the music.

Beside him, she crossed her arms, shifting from one foot to the other. Could everyone else in the room feel the tension between them?

He cleared his throat. "Okay, there's Dillon at the bar and us talking to him."

Cash explained to Overstreet and Watts how Dillon had claimed he'd broken up with Laurel and didn't know where she was.

They surveyed the screen as Dillon moved through the club, speaking to a few people, mostly women. His charm and looks obviously worked for him as most of the women he approached seemed to reciprocate his interest.

"Creep," Maya muttered under her breath.

Cash agreed. He'd love to find something on this guy that would stick and get him off the streets. Dillon Cordell was a predator, no doubt about it.

"Okay, there." He paused the recording. "That's her, right?"

Maya nodded. "I think so. Same hair color and length. Same build. Red dress."

Dillon approached the young woman sitting at the bar, and two engaged in a conversation. It looked friendly, as the woman laughed and swatted at Dillon playfully.

"Check that out," he said.

"What's he doing?" Watts leaned in.

The young woman turned away from Dillon to speak to another woman on the other side of her. Dillon opened his jacket and took something out, but it was hard to tell what.

"You think he put something in her drink?" Maya asked.

"The camera angle doesn't show a good view of her glass, though," Cash said. "But if he did, that was the perfect opportunity."

They watched more of the footage, and the young woman had a few more drinks. Soon, her behavior changed, and she began to lean on Dillon and sway in her seat.

"She's either drunk or drugged," Maya said.

Anger churned in Cash's gut. The bar area was crowded, but no one seemed to notice what was happening right in front of them as Dillon helped the woman off the stool and led her toward the door.

How many other young women had Dillon preyed on? And what had happened to them?

Cash itched to get his hands on the guy.

"Got 'em." Chandler slapped the table. "Driver's licenses and addresses for the three women's names we got from the patrons."

Overstreet reached for his phone. "Give me the info, and I'll get Dansby's police chief on it."

Cash breathed a sigh of relief. The Dansby PD would get officers dispatched to each address to search for the woman. If things went well, they could have Dillon Cordell in custody tonight.

Maya unlocked her front door and dropped her bag in the foyer. Anger coursed through her system, sending currents of electricity through her veins.

They didn't have Dillon. They hadn't found the young woman he left with. And they were no closer to finding Laurel than they had been this morning.

Behind her, Cash closed the door, then pushed past her. "I said, let me go first."

He entered her living room, gun in hand but holding it down by his side.

After they'd returned to the GBI office with SAC Overstreet, they'd checked in with Addie, who had left Cash's truck at the lab. With no vehicle of his own in working order, Cash had borrowed a sedan and driven her home. But he'd insisted on coming in with her to check her house.

"I can clear my own place," she said.

He turned, his jaw tight. "I don't care, Maya. Let me do it."

She met his stare, but instead of anger, she saw fear. He was scared for her. He wanted to protect her.

Her stomach flipped, but she nodded. "Fine."

She was too tired to argue anyway. Arms folded, she waited

in the foyer as he went through her house. Invasion of privacy aside, it was weird having Cash in her home. He'd never stepped farther than the doorway when they were dating, and now he was checking every nook and cranny. She mentally inventoried her rooms, trying to remember if she'd made her bed this morning and put away the laundry.

Not that she could do anything about it now.

He returned to the foyer after a few minutes and clipped his firearm back into its holster. "All clear."

Leaving her bag where it was, she walked into the den. Cash followed. His presence seemed to take up all the space in the room.

Was he going to stand there all night?

"I wish you had an alarm system." He glanced around.

"My landlord won't allow them. Too many get tripped by mistake and bother the neighbors." She shrugged. "I've never had any issues before."

He opened his mouth but then closed it again.

She understood what he didn't say. She'd never had someone try to kill her before.

Memories of the past few days rushed back, and she shivered. "Well, thanks for checking my house."

"Thanks for letting me."

She couldn't help the smile that tugged at her lips.

"I'd better get going," he said.

Maya rubbed her arms. "I wish…"

Cash stepped closer. "We're going to catch him. It's only a matter of time."

"Sure." But she wasn't convinced.

Dansby PD had sent officers to each address of the women identified at the club, but no sign of Dillon. Two of the women were accounted for. One had been at the club but claimed not to know Dillon. Nor had she showed any signs of being drugged or inebriated. The other had been at her job at a local grocery store, and her alibi was confirmed.

The third woman, Kellie Ryles, wasn't at home, but since she lived alone, there was no way to know where she was.

Cash's piercing gaze held her in place. "We've done all we can for tonight. Dansby PD is sitting on Kellie's place all night in case she returns. Overstreet has Chandler working to get her phone number. Once he gets that, we'll do an emergency trace on it to see if we can find her. And the BOLO is still out for Dillon's car. Something will pop soon."

She wanted to believe him, but her hope was dwindling.

He took her hands in his, and a different kind of electricity flowed up her arms.

"Try to get some sleep," he said. "It's been a long night and an even longer day."

A long couple of days. Her body ached. And so did her soul.

For a moment, she wanted nothing more than to be encircled in Cash's arms again, lean on his chest and absorb his strength.

Their eyes met, and he held her gaze, something unreadable there.

Then, he stepped away. "I—I'll call you tomorrow."

She followed him to the foyer. "Unless something happens tonight. Then you'll let me know, right?"

He turned, hand on the doorknob. "Yes, I promise." Opening the door, he surveyed her parking lot. "Pendleton PD will keep watch again tonight."

The feeling of security washed over her once more. She wasn't used to being looked out for, cared for.

And she was terrified of getting used to it.

Cash glanced her way one more time. "Lock this."

She resisted the urge to roll her eyes. "Of course."

And then he left. She closed and locked the door, then watched through the peephole as he strode to his borrowed sedan, lifting a hand to the Pendleton officer nearby.

Her apartment felt hollow without him.

Stop it.

She was not going to get used to having Cash around.

The day was catching up to her. Fatigue pulled at her body, but her mind continued to whirl. She wasn't going to be able to sleep anytime soon. She was too wired. And too worried.

Going to the kitchen, she turned the kettle on and opened the honey and jar of loose-leaf chamomile tea she kept on the counter. Her remedy for sleepless nights.

She poured the tea and settled on the couch, clicked on the television and chose an old black-and-white movie. One she knew all the lines for. Pulling a fluffy blanket over her legs, she nestled into the couch cushions and sipped her tea.

The movie had barely started when she began feeling the effects of the drink. Relaxation began to flow over her. Then, a wave of dizziness.

Wait. Maya sat up, and the room spun. She grabbed her head.

She'd never had this kind of reaction to her chamomile before. It usually relaxed her and helped calm her nerves.

Nausea hit. She tried to get up from the couch, but her muscles didn't want to cooperate. Why couldn't she move? The empty teacup fell from her hands and dropped to the rug.

What was wrong? Her mind felt foggy. Thick.

And so did her chest. Her lungs were heavy, and she couldn't get a full breath.

Something wasn't right.

Think, Maya. She commanded her brain to work, but it didn't respond. Help. She needed help. Call…someone. Who?

Darkness seeped into the edges of her vision.

Stay awake. Breathe. Why was it so hard to do?

Her phone. Where?

She found it in her lap. Pressed the screen. Her vision blurred. She tried to focus.

More fog.

She pressed a number. Then everything went dark.

SEVEN

Cash pressed the button on the sedan's console to disconnect the call. He'd left Maya's apartment and started for home, but something kept niggling at the back of his mind. Something was bothering him, and he wouldn't be able to sleep until he'd followed up on it.

An idea had formed, and he'd called Noah Chandler to meet back at the GBI office. Cash would need Noah's help to figure out if his hunch had legs.

Something else was bothering him, too, and it wasn't only the events of tonight.

The image of Maya's hesitation tonight flashed through his mind. He'd asked her to trust him, and he'd seen the war going on in her expression. When she'd finally put her hand in his, he had been flooded with relief. He hadn't wanted to leave her to chase the shooter.

He recalled the feeling of holding her in his arms tonight at the club. The vulnerability in her eyes when she'd talked about her mother's overdose and then losing her sister.

The way his heart beat a little faster when she was around. And how he wanted more than anything to wipe away the hurt he could see in her eyes.

The fear of losing Maya was almost equal to his fear of losing himself and falling completely head over heels for her.

But he'd had his shot with Maya, and he'd blown it. Thrown

her into the same category as all the other woman he'd dated. And pushed her away like he had everyone else.

The truth was, Maya wasn't like any other woman he knew. And if he let himself, he could imagine spending a lifetime with her.

His phone lit up in the dash holder. Maya's number flashed on the screen. A trickle of worry flared, but the deputy was right outside her place. And he'd made sure all the doors and windows were locked.

Maybe she had a question or had thought of some information that might help in the search.

He clicked the button to answer. "Hi, Maya."

She didn't answer.

"Hello?"

No response.

"Maya? Maya!" The trickle of worry became a full-fledged fire as he spun the car around, clicking on the flashing lights and siren.

He could hear what sounded like the television in the background, but no response from her. Pressing the gas pedal, he sped down the road to her neighborhood.

He couldn't risk hanging up with her to call the Pendleton deputy.

"Maya, can you hear me? Hang on. I'm on my way."

The ten-minute drive felt like an hour. Finally, he roared into her parking lot and pulled up beside the deputy. The officer jumped out of his vehicle as Cash opened the door of his sedan.

"What's wrong?" he asked.

Cash made a beeline for Maya's door. "I don't know. She called but she isn't saying anything."

The deputy followed him up the sidewalk and to her front stoop.

Banging on the door, Cash shouted her name. "Maya? It's Cash. Open the door."

Lights came on in the townhouse next door, but he didn't care if he woke the whole neighborhood.

No answer. And no time for waiting.

"Stand back," he said to the deputy. "I'm going to try to break the door in."

The young officer's eyes went wide as Cash backed up a few steps then rushed toward the door, throwing his weight against it. The doorframe cracked but didn't open.

His body protested, but he backed up and ran at the door again. This time, the frame splintered, and Cash stumbled inside.

"Maya?" He ran through the foyer into the living room. A couple of lamps were on as well as the television.

Then he saw her. In a heap on the floor next to the sofa. Not moving.

Cash rushed to her side. Her phone lay near her hand, the call still connected to his phone. He turned her slightly so he could see her face. Unconscious but no visible signs of injury. Shaking her gently, he called her name again. No response. He pressed fingers against her neck. Pressed harder. Finally, he felt a pulse. Weak. Slow.

Tilting her head back, he checked her breathing. Barely perceptible. But there.

"Call for an ambulance!" he shouted to the deputy. The officer obeyed, keying his radio to call it in.

Cash glanced at the back door. No sign of forced entry, other than the front door he had broken. Nothing near Maya other than an empty teacup.

Her skin was pale and clammy. Lips tinged a slight shade of blue.

Terror split his chest. He recognized the signs. An overdose.

"Hey," he called to the officer. "Narcan. Do you have any?"

"Yeah, in my car."

"Get it now. She's overdosing."

Please, God. Please.

He rubbed Maya's arms, trying to wake her up. "Come on, honey. Breathe. Keep breathing."

An overdose caused the brain to stop sending signals to the body to breathe. If she stopped, he could start CPR, but for now he needed to encourage her body to do it on her own.

The officer ran into the room and handed him the small bottle of nose spray. The emergency drug naloxone should reverse the effects of the overdose and cause Maya's brain to wake up.

He administered the drug by inserting the nozzle into her nostril and pressing.

And waited.

"Please wake up, please. Come on." His own heart pounded a fast rhythm in his chest.

Her body convulsed as she took a breath. Her eyelids fluttered.

Thank You, God.

Cash held her face. "Hey, take it easy. I'm here. I've got you."

The sound of sirens floated on the air as the ambulance approached.

"Wha…" She tried to talk, but he pressed a finger to her lips.

"It's okay. You're okay. Just breathe." His own chest ached as he took in air and held her hand.

The paramedics came in and loaded her onto the gurney.

Cash turned to the Pendleton deputy. "I'm going to follow the ambulance to the hospital. I need you to secure the scene until my team can get here."

He nodded and Cash followed the paramedics as they took Maya out and loaded her into the back of the ambulance.

In his sedan, he dialed SAC Overstreet. "Sir, we've got a situation." Someone had tried to kill Maya. Again. And they were still no closer to finding out who.

An incessant noise made its way into Maya's mind. A beeping sound. She looked for a way to stop it but found none. *Wake up.* She needed to wake up. Stop the noise.

Opening her eyes, she tried to focus. Beige walls. Soft lights. Machines on each side of her.

She was not in her bedroom.

As awareness slowly seeped into her mind, she took stock. Hospital room. She was in the hospital. Cool oxygen flowed from the tube in her nostrils.

How did she get here?

The last thing she remembered was…home. Her living room. The sofa. Watching a movie. Black-and-white. Warmth. Coziness. A cup of tea. And then…

She took a deep breath as the memory washed over her. She'd struggled to breathe. To move. To think. Tried to call for help—

Her eyes landed on Cash. Asleep in a chair next to her bed. His head was cocked to the side at an uncomfortable angle. A five o'clock shadow peppered his jaw. Hair mussed.

And a book rested on his chest. She focused on it.

The Bible? Well, that was new. The Cash she'd known two years ago hadn't been one for religion.

But he was different now. She could see it. He had changed. Since this whole ordeal had started, Cash had been helpful, kind and protective. He'd saved her life more than once.

Yet, she wasn't sure that proved enough to risk opening her heart to him once more. Besides, she had no idea if his feelings toward her had changed at all.

She glanced down at her arm. Tubes ran from the IV port in the crook of her elbow.

And Cash's fingers rested on hers.

Warmth spread as tears sprang to her eyes.

She reached her other hand to her cheek to swipe them away, and the bed creaked slightly.

Cash's eyelids opened and he sat up, looking around. His gaze met hers, and a flurry of emotions floated on his face. Emotions flooded through her as well.

"You're awake." He smiled, and butterflies danced in her stomach.

"How—" She tried to speak, but her throat cracked. Swallowing felt like eating a handful of dust.

"Wait." Cash stood and set the Bible down, then picked up a cup from the table near her bed. He poured water from the small bottle, then slipped a straw into the cup. He brought it over to her and pressed the button on the remote to raise the head of her bed. Then, he held the cup and straw while she took a drink. "Easy. Small sips."

She wanted to gulp the whole thing, but as the liquid traveled to her stomach, she thought better of it. Best to spare Cash the vision of her throwing up.

The water helped her throat, and she lay back on the pillows. "Thank you."

He nodded, returning the cup to the table.

"What time is it?" she asked.

He checked his watch. "Quarter after two."

She tried to calculate. Cash had dropped her off at home around midnight. Was that a couple of hours ago? Sunshine filtered through the blinds over the window. How was it light outside?

"The better question," he said, "is what day is it?"

"What?"

"You've been out for almost fourteen hours."

"I...have?" Confusion swirled in her brain, along with a low ache. She rubbed her forehead. "You've been here the whole time?"

Ducking his head, Cash nodded, not meeting her eyes. "Yeah."

He'd come to her rescue. He'd been standing guard.

Her heart ached, but she pushed the feelings aside. "What happened?"

He sat on the edge of her bed, taking her hand again. Gentle. Comforting.

"You…well, you overdosed."

Shock ran through her. "No, I…couldn't have. I've never—"

"I know. You didn't do it. Someone drugged you."

"How?"

He sighed. "It was your tea."

"It was regular chamomile. Organic, from a local shop."

"From what we can tell, someone laced the jar with crushed opioids."

She shook her head. None of this made sense. "I drink it all the time."

"We think it was recent, based on your reaction to it. The consensus is someone dosed the jar maybe a few hours before we got to your place." His brows pulled together. "It wouldn't take much snooping in your life to know it would be a good way to hurt you."

"I rave about it all the time on social media." She lay back on the pillows as she processed what he'd said. "How did they get into my house?"

Cash's eyes narrowed. "We had a deputy watching you, but we didn't have anyone guarding your home while you were away at the club."

She knew that look. Cash was blaming himself for the fact that someone broke into her home and contaminated her favorite tea. "That's not your fault."

He shook off her words of comfort. "Addie's been working the scene since she finished processing my truck last night. She found residue in your cup first, and then she traced it back to the jar of tea." He frowned. "She also found a bag of illegal pills in your bathroom cabinet."

She sucked in a breath, bolting upright. "Those aren't mine. I didn't—"

He held up a hand. "We know, Maya. They had to be planted by the same person who drugged your tea."

"What proof do you have?"

He looked away for a moment. "Well, nothing conclusive right now. But we'll find it."

Or she could be charged with possession.

Fresh tears flooded her eyes. Too many to stop.

"Hey." Cash rubbed a thumb across her hand. "We trust you. We'll find a way to prove it. You have no history of drug abuse."

"But I do."

"What?" His brows rose.

Despair lay like a brick in her gut. "My mother had an addiction. My sister has an addiction." She looked at Cash. "Who's to say I don't?"

"I say." His jaw hardened. "And Owen says. And Addie. We know you, Maya. You don't have a drug problem. And if it comes down to it, we'll all testify to that fact."

"Good afternoon." A man entered her room. Clean-cut and dressed in a doctor's white coat, he looked to be in his forties. His expression lightened when he saw Maya. "Well, looks like someone has decided to join us."

"She woke up maybe five minutes ago," Cash said.

The man nodded and stepped to her bed, extending a hand. "I'm Dr. Greene. It's nice to finally meet you, Miss Reid."

She shook his hand. Cash held up his phone and pointed to the hall, then slipped out while Dr. Greene explained more about what had happened to her as he took her vitals and recorded everything in his tablet.

The Narcan that Cash had administered had done its job of restoring her breathing and heartbeat, but the opioids had sent her body into shock, which had caused unconsciousness. They'd also kept her on oxygen and a heart monitor to watch for any recurrence of respiratory or cardiac distress.

Dr. Greene checked the readouts on her monitors. "Looks

like you are stabilizing well and on your way back to normal." He smiled. "Let's try taking you off the oxygen and let you breathe on your own. Make sure your O2 levels stay up." He removed the tubing from her nose, then pressed his stethoscope against her chest. "Take some deep breaths for me."

She inhaled, happy when her lungs filled with air.

The doctor listened and nodded. "Sounds good." He patted her hand. "We'll keep monitoring your O2 levels for a few hours, but things are progressing in the right direction. Barring any problems, we should be able to release you this evening."

He left, and Maya lay back on the pillows, enjoying the feeling of moving her lungs, of air passing in and out of her body.

Between almost drowning in the lake and the overdose, she never wanted to experience the feeling of not being able to breathe again.

Cash stepped back into the room, tucking the phone into his pocket. The expression on his face threatened to take her breath away once more.

"What is it?" Maya looked up at him from her hospital bed.

Cash did not want to tell her what he'd just found out while the doctor was assessing her. She'd looked so hopeful earlier. And now, that lost look had returned to her eyes. Fear had replaced her peace.

And what he had to say was only going to make that worse.

"Did they…" She swallowed. "Did they find Laurel?" The words whispered from her lips.

"No," he rushed to reassure her. "Well, maybe. It's kind of a yes and no situation."

"What? Cash, tell me." Frustration lined her face.

He settled onto the side of her bed again, praying for the words. "Last night, after I dropped you off at your house, I called Noah Chandler. After we watched Dillon leave the club with that young woman, I started thinking he was mixed up in something more than drugs."

Wariness crept into her eyes. She could probably guess where he was going with this.

"So," he said, "I had Chandler start checking the dark web. See if we could find anything connecting Dillon to Elizabeth Fielding and our new missing woman. And Laurel."

"You're thinking..." She let her words trail off.

He nodded. "Human trafficking."

"Did you find anything?"

"Sort of. Nothing connecting Dillon to Elizabeth Fielding. And it's probably too soon to find anything on the new missing woman."

"And... Laurel?"

"Nothing concrete. Chandler contacted an agent he knows with the FBI and told him what we're working on. They ran the names of a couple of other missing persons over the past year. And he found a...site. No pictures, but there are descriptions of young women who are...available." The words boiled like bile down his throat. Selling another human being was one of the most reprehensible practices he could imagine. "There was one description that sounded a lot like Laurel."

Her hand went to her throat, fresh tears springing to her eyes.

It was killing Cash to be the one to bring her this news. The only solace he had was if he could find her sister.

"You think Dillon is behind this?"

He nodded. "I don't think he's the mastermind, but he's definitely involved somehow. From the way he picked up that woman at the club, I think he could be the bait that lures them in. Noah's been working all night, and he was finally able to get through the encryption and confirm the IP address. It traced back to Dillon's building. That's what Noah called to tell me. We've got enough for a search warrant now, and it should be ready within the hour."

"That fast?"

"Given the circumstances, SAC Overstreet had it fast-tracked. The team is gearing up to raid Dillon's apartment. And I'm going with them. I'll arrange for an officer—"

Maya sat up and moved to the side of the bed.

"What are you doing?" Cash asked.

"I'm coming with you."

"Absolutely not. You're in no shape to—"

She glared up at him, fire in her eyes. "He might have Laurel. I cannot sit here and wonder."

"I can't let you do that."

Maya's eyes pleaded with him. "Please, Cash. I have to be there."

Everything in him said no, but he couldn't deny her this. He sighed. "All right, but only if the doctor signs off. And you stay in the car until we've cleared the building."

She held up two fingers. "Scout's honor."

He doubted she would hold to that, but if he didn't take her, she would find a way to get there on her own. An unknown factor that could prove more dangerous. For the team and for her.

An hour later, he pulled up to a store parking lot a block from Dillon's apartment. His team had set up there to prepare for the raid. They would go in stealth so as not to tip Dillon off or send him running.

Maya, pale but determined, sat in his passenger seat.

He was surprised Dr. Greene had agreed to release her, but maybe the doc had got the idea she wouldn't take no for an answer either.

"Stay here," he said. "I'll check in with the SAC and get the plan."

"And you'll let me know?" The despair in her eyes cut into him.

"As much as I can."

He approached the group huddled around SAC Overstreet's sedan.

Owen tipped his head as Cash approached. "Is that Maya in your car?"

"Yeah."

"Should she be out here?"

He leveled a gaze at Owen. "As if I had a choice."

His partner gave him a knowing grin. "Of course."

"How is she?" Addie asked.

"Not firing on all eight cylinders yet but getting there."

Addie shook her head. "I'm so glad she's okay. And thankful you got there in time."

So was he. The alternative would've been…

He wouldn't let himself go there.

Focusing on Overstreet, he listened as the SAC laid out the game plan. They would approach in teams, one at each entrance to the apartment building. Converge on Dillon's apartment and keep at least one team on the ground in case he went out the fire escape.

"We want him alive, people," Overstreet said. "He's our best prospect for finding Laurel DeWitt and any others."

Cash returned to his car and opened the trunk to extract his tactical gear. Maya opened the passenger door and swung her legs out but stayed seated.

She was trying. He'd give her that. The urge to vest up and storm the building had to be strong.

He gave her a brief overview of the plan.

"And you'll let me know if you find Laurel, right?" she asked.

He pointed to the mic at his shoulder. "Same channel as my car's radio. You'll hear everything I hear."

She nodded. "Thanks, Cash."

It was the least he could do. The best would be to find her sister and deliver her safely to Maya.

His radio crackled.

Dansby PD's dispatcher came over the line. "Attention all units. Be advised. Suspect Dillon Cordell has been spotted. Repeat, suspect has been spotted. Last seen in the 1000 block of Sunset Avenue, headed north, in a Chevrolet Camaro. License plate…"

Cash slammed his trunk and jumped in the car, throwing his vest into the back seat. "He's running." He shifted into Drive and took off, heading down the block toward Dillon's apartment.

"How did he know?"

"No idea. But if he's running, he's got a reason."

Other GBI sedans joined in behind him, lights and sirens blaring. A couple of Dansby black-and-whites came in from other roads. Cash kept his eyes out for the Camaro as information continued to come in from dispatch.

He sped down Sunset and turned right onto Garden Boulevard as the latest information had Dillon heading north. Out of town. He could be headed to where he was keeping the women. Or he could be leading them away.

Either way, Dillon Cordell wasn't getting away from them this time.

Cash downshifted as a delivery truck pulled into the intersection and swerved around him.

Maya gripped the seat but kept silent.

Two more turns and Cash headed into a neighborhood road. His gut clenched as he kept watch. Residential areas meant more people, and more chances for someone to get hurt.

"Turn here." Maya pointed to a side road to his left.

"Dispatch said he was on Evergreen."

"Yeah, but that leads to Highway 215."

"Which leads to the interstate. He's trying to get to the freeway."

"And this is a short cut." She held up her phone with a maps app opened.

He slowed down, hesitating.

"Trust me, Cash."

Nodding, he turned left as the other sedans flew past him.

Maya's shortcut took them behind a strip mall. Cash sped around the corner.

"There he is!" She pointed to the other end of the lot.

The orange Camaro disappeared around another set of buildings.

Cash relayed their location to dispatch and floored it to the other end of the line of buildings.

Sliding around the corner, he slammed on his brakes. "Dead end."

In the corner, he spied the edge of the Camaro.

"Stay here," he ordered Maya as he exited his car. Gun drawn, he eased around a dumpster and started toward Dillon's car. "Dillon Cordell, exit the car with your hands up."

The windows of the Camaro were too dark to see inside. He couldn't tell whether Dillon had a weapon.

Cash found cover behind a set of pallets. "Come on, man. It's over. No way out. Give up."

Movement to his right. He shifted his gaze from Dillon's car to see Maya making her way from the opposite side. She was heading toward Dillon's vehicle.

What was she doing?

So much for staying in the car.

No weapon. And no protective gear. She was a sitting duck if Dillon had a gun.

Gritting his teeth, Cash eased away from his cover and shifted toward Maya. They were going to have words after this was over.

They were a good fifty yards from the Camaro when Cash reached her. He grabbed her arm. "Get back to the car. Now."

She turned.

"I can—"

The world shifted as a loud boom echoed in the alley. He

fell backward, pulling Maya with him beside the building as debris fell around them.

He sat up, eyes searching.

Dillon Cordell's car was a ball of fire.

EIGHT

Maya dabbed at her face with the rough paper towel in the gas station's bathroom, washing away the dirt and ash from the car explosion. She and Cash had been protected from the worst of the blast by the dumpster and small overhang of the building.

And then the scene had been overtaken by GBI agents, local police, fire trucks and ambulances.

After getting checked out by the paramedics, she'd retreated to the bathroom at the nearby gas station, needing a moment to compose herself.

Other than a few scrapes and bruises, which she would be feeling tomorrow, they'd escaped the explosion in one piece.

The same couldn't be said for Dillon Cordell.

She leaned against the sink, willing her hands to stop shaking. Loss of life in any form was horrible. But her heart ached at yet another setback. Dillon had been their only lead and the last link to where her sister could be.

The door opened, and Addie King's head popped around. "Hey, just checking if you needed anything."

Maya smiled at the agent, who was quickly becoming one of her favorite people. "I'm good." She looked down at her clothes, soiled with dirt and ash. "At least we were far enough away to only get knocked down."

She needed to start carrying another set of clothing everywhere she went. But since they'd come directly from the hospital to the raid on Dillon's apartment, she hadn't had time to go home and pick up anything.

Addie surveyed her. "You don't look too bad, considering. It could have been much worse." She tipped her head, concern written on her face. "How do you feel?"

Desperate? Tired? Hopeless?

Maya shrugged. "Like I've been drugged and then almost blown up."

Laughter bubbled up at the ridiculousness of the past two days, and she couldn't help the chuckle that escaped. Addie joined her, and the camaraderie felt good.

"Oh, hon." Addie gave her a quick hug. "You've really been through it, haven't you? Here," She handed Maya a protein bar and a bottle of juice. "I thought you could use something to counteract the adrenaline crash."

Maya took the food, giving Addie's hand a squeeze. "Thank you."

They left the restroom and exited the gas station.

She opened the bar and took a few bites, then washed it down with the juice.

"Cash called," Addie said. "Dillon's apartment is clear if you want to take a look."

While the fire department worked on putting out the flames consuming the remains of Dillon's car, Cash had joined Overstreet and Owen as they checked out Dillon's apartment.

She paused mid-bite. "Did they find…anyone?" It was almost too much to hope that Laurel would be in Dillon's apartment, waiting to be found.

Addie shook her head. "Place was empty. But Cash wants you to take a look and see if you can connect anything in the apartment with your sister."

"Let's go."

They drove back to the apartment building in Addie's car. Cash was waiting for them in the lobby.

"Here." He handed Maya paper shoe covers and a pair of latex gloves while they ascended the stairs to the second floor. "Forensics is still processing the place, but I wanted to let you take a look before everything gets bagged up and sent to the lab."

They entered the apartment, and Maya glanced around. The converted loft had an open layout, with a leather sectional and large television separating the living area from the adjacent kitchen with high-end appliances and expensive finishings.

She let out a low whistle. "Nice digs for a mechanic."

"Exactly," Cash said. "See anything that could be Laurel's?"

Maya examined various items on bookshelves, then opened cabinets. "Nothing so far."

"How about you?" Addie asked Cash. "Anything popping in that memory of yours?"

He shook his head.

Owen slapped him playfully on the back. "That's some hard head you've got if even an explosion couldn't knock anything loose in there."

His partner's teasing was meant to lighten the mood, she could tell. But from the way Cash's hands fisted and his jaw twitched, it hadn't helped.

"Let's check out the bedroom and bathroom," Cash said, leading her away. But not before she caught the look Owen and Addie shared.

They were worried about their friend.

She was, too.

Wait. Had she just thought of Cash Brenner as her friend?

Glancing at him as he walked through Dillon's bedroom, she realized it was true. He wasn't only some guy she'd gone out with, or even some GBI agent who was helping with her case.

She cared about him. And in a way that made her cheeks pink and her heart thump.

When had that happened? Had it been when he'd rescued

her from drowning in the lake? Or saved her from dying of an overdose? Or protected her from a car explosion?

No. All of those things were heroic. Absolutely. But that was Cash. It was who he was.

And she'd always admired that about him. Never stopped. Even after he'd broken up with her and walked away from what could have become something special.

The Cash she was starting to see now, though, was different. His protectiveness, his caring. Like the other night, when he'd tried to reassure her that God was fighting for them. His confidence in something bigger than himself.

"Anything?" He'd caught her staring at him.

Heat rushed up her neck, and she blinked. "Sorry, I was lost in thought."

"About?"

An idea struck. "What about his computer?" If Noah had been able to find the site on the dark web where Dillon was… auctioning— The thought turned her stomach. But there had to be a computer somewhere that Dillon used to run his business.

Cash pointed to a desk outside the room. "Missing."

"What?" She went out to the desk area. Dust covered the back half of the surface, with wires disconnected.

"Looks like this was where he kept a laptop, but it's gone. Either whoever rigged his car took it, or he had it with him when he fled."

"So, it would've been in the car when…"

"Yeah."

"Could it have survived?"

"Doubtful, but if there's anything left, we'll find it at the lab. And if not, someone else has it."

Once the fire department had put out the flames, the vehicle would be loaded onto a truck and taken to the GBI lab.

Another thought struck, and she gasped. "The DeWitts. We need to let them know about Dillon."

He nodded. "Before they hear it from the media. Pendleton PD are making the notification to Dillon's family, but we can take care of the DeWitts."

"I'd like to check in with Helene, too."

"I'll drive."

Cash pulled into the circular drive of the DeWitts' home. "Wow," he said, turning to Maya in the passenger seat. "You weren't kidding."

She'd filled him in on Laurel's adoptive family as he drove to Orchard Park. Their business, neighborhood and lifestyle. But he wasn't quite prepared for the DeWitts' home. The two-story brick house and expansive, landscaped yard spoke of wealth. Not old money, but not new money either. Well-established money. That was what he'd go with.

She nodded and got out of the car. He joined her as they went up the short walk to the stone steps. She rang the bell. Her expression was unreadable, but tension rolled off her.

He didn't have time to ask before the door opened. A sturdy woman with short gray hair answered the door.

"Ilsa?" Maya asked.

The woman narrowed her eyes, taking them both in. "Yes?"

"It's Maya Reid. We spoke on the phone last week."

"Ah, yes. I remember," Ilsa said, her thick German accent coloring her words. "Have you found the girl?"

Maya's face fell, her shoulders slumped. "No. Not…yet. But I do have news for the DeWitts. Are they home?"

"Missus is in. Come." She opened the door, and they followed her across the large foyer into a parlor. Two cream-colored sofas sat opposite each other. "Sit." Ilsa pointed to one and waited.

Maya sat, and Cash joined her.

He got the feeling Ilsa wouldn't leave the room until he did.

"I'll get her."

As Ilsa disappeared down the hall, Cash turned to Maya. "Who was that?"

"The housekeeper."

"But she didn't recognize you."

"Oh, right. I didn't meet her last time. Wade's secretary answered the door that day. Andrea? No, Audra…something. I wrote it in my notes…which were in my SUV."

Which had gone into the lake.

She frowned, the memory disturbing to both of them.

"Maya?" A petite blonde entered the room and made a beeline for Maya, as they both stood to greet her.

"Hello, Mrs. DeWitt."

"Helene, dear. Is there any news?" Mrs. DeWitt took one look at Maya, and concern flared in her eyes. "Are you all right?"

They'd come straight from Dillon's apartment, not taking time to clean up or change. Not that Maya could've gone home. Her apartment was still a crime scene, the front door boarded up from where he'd broken it down last night to get to her.

The image of her lying on the floor, barely breathing, barreled into him. If she hadn't been able to dial his number, if he hadn't been close enough, if the Pendleton officer hadn't had the Narcan… Too many ifs for comfort.

But Maya was alive for one reason. God's mercy.

He tuned in as Maya explained what had happened to Dillon. She left out the parts where they'd both been nearly killed more than once.

"Oh, dear." Mrs. DeWitt paled and slid onto a nearby chair. Hand at her throat, she absently fingered a strand of pearls around her neck. "How positively awful."

Maya resumed her seat on the sofa, waiting for Mrs. DeWitt to process the news.

She looked up. "But what about Laurel? If he's…gone, what does that mean for finding my daughter?"

Maya had been right about Mrs. DeWitt's concern for her

daughter. Her eyes wide, the older woman looked at them with fear and hope.

Cash sat next to Maya on the couch. "We're still searching for Laurel. We have a few avenues we're investigating, although Dillon Cordell was our best lead."

Mrs. DeWitt blinked, seeming to notice him for the first time. "I'm sorry. I don't believe we've been introduced."

He stood and held out a hand, which she took with delicate fingers. "Special Agent Cash Brenner. I'm working with Maya on this investigation."

"Nice to meet you." She nodded. "So, what do you mean by avenues?"

"I can't go into details as this is still an active investigation. But I would like to ask you a few questions, to clarify what we've gathered so far."

"Of course. Anything I can do to help."

"Can you tell us how Laurel met Dillon?"

She waved a hand. "Oh, one of those school functions. I can't remember exactly."

Skylar Hudson had said it was at a party, but Laurel had probably censored that information for her mother.

"And how long did they date before Laurel disappeared?"

"Let's see. They were dating last Christmas. I remember Laurel texting him while we were in Vale. We always go during the holidays."

"Is that when Laurel got injured?" Maya asked.

Helene's brow creased. "How did you know about that?"

"We talked to Skylar," Maya said. "She told us that Laurel had hurt her back on that trip."

"Yes, she took a tumble on the slopes. Pulled a few muscles in her back. So strange."

"How so?" he asked.

"Laurel has been skiing since she could walk, practically. I've never seen her fall like that. She said one of the straps on her skis broke, but they were brand-new. That shouldn't have happened." She shook her head. "If Laurel hadn't been as adept as she was, it could have been much worse."

"Fatal?" Was there more to this than an accident?

Mrs. DeWitt looked up at him. "Yes, I believe it could have been." Her expression dropped. "That's when she started taking those pain pills. I had no idea it would lead to—" Her chin trembled.

Maya moved to sit next to her, taking her hand. "How could you have known?"

"I supposed I couldn't have. But still, Laurel is my child. I should've spoken up when I first noticed something was off."

"What did you notice?" Cash asked.

"Laurel seemed preoccupied right before the end of the semester. I chalked it up to the stress of school, finals. But then, she met Dillon, and she seemed so excited about the relationship. But once we returned home, she started to become distant. Not calling or answering my calls. No visits on the weekends. She began to drift away from us. And then…she disappeared." Tears flooded her eyes.

He stepped to a side table nearby and retrieved a box of tissues, handing them to Maya. She took a few and gave them to Mrs. DeWitt.

While she took a moment to compose herself, Cash walked around the room, surveying the photos in frames on the tables and shelves. Laurel was the prominent subject, from toddler through childhood to teen years. Seemingly every important milestone and achievement in Laurel's life was documented in pictures.

It was clear the DeWitts doted on their only child and had showered her with every opportunity possible for a young woman growing into high-class society. Tennis lessons. Horseback riding. And—

He stumbled as his eyes caught on another photo, and a

slice of fear shot through him. Lights danced in his vision, his breath hitching.

"Cash? You okay?" Maya's voice sounded far away. Hollow.

His ears rang.

"Um… I, uh…" He turned toward the door. "Mind if I use your restroom?"

"Second door on the left," Mrs. DeWitt's voice followed him into the hall.

He barely registered the directions, but as he staggered down the hallway, he saw the open door of a powder room and went inside, closing the door behind him. He leaned against the wall, sweat popping out on his forehead.

Dark visions danced across his mind, muddled and unclear. But the feeling of fear was unmistakable. Cash closed his eyes, trying to retrieve the memory, to bring the images into focus.

He was running. In the dark. But he had to get away. Something was chasing him. Dangerous and fast. A deep growl. Snarling. Sharp teeth at his heels.

Run. Go. Get out. The commands shot through his brain. He had to get away from the animal chasing him.

He could see it clearly. A dog. Large, lean. And coming for him.

Cash strained, willing his mind to see it.

A Doberman. Black. With a golden collar on its neck.

The same kind he'd seen in a photo in the DeWitts' living room.

Maya took the cup of tea Ilsa offered from a silver tray. The delicate bone china felt like it could disintegrate in her hand at any moment.

The scent of jasmine floated from the brew, but after her disaster with the chamomile tea, she wasn't sure she wanted to take a drink. It might be a while before she could enjoy tea again.

Not wanting to appear rude, Maya pretended to take a sip and then deposited the cup onto the tray Ilsa had set on the coffee table.

Helene held her cup in her hands, taking small sips. "I picked up an affinity for jasmine tea during one of our trips to China. It helps to calm my nerves."

She wished she could assure Mrs. DeWitt that they were going to find Laurel and bring her home. But after losing their only lead in Dillon Cordell, she was beginning to lose hope herself.

"Did Laurel ever mention any of Dillon's friends? Someone he worked with, perhaps?" Maya asked.

"No, I don't believe she did. At least, not anyone I can recall." She set her cup down. "Do you believe Dillon actually had something to do with Laurel's disappearance?"

"He was a person of interest, certainly." She kept things purposefully vague.

She believed Dillon had everything to do with Laurel's disappearance, but she hesitated to share what they'd found on the dark web. She wasn't sure how much she could tell Helene without compromising any important information.

Best to let Cash take the lead in those matters.

Maya glanced toward the hall. He had been in the bathroom for a few minutes. Should she check on him? He'd seemed unwell, maybe a bit agitated, when he left the room.

Footsteps sounded, and then Cash entered the room, his face pale. Without a word, he walked to one of the shelves surrounding the fireplace and picked up a silver frame. He brought it to the couch and showed it to Helene.

Maya didn't miss the slight tremor in his left hand as he passed over the picture.

"Are these your dogs?" he asked.

"Yes," she answered. "Well, they're Wade's. He raises them

as show dogs." She turned the frame so Maya could see a teenaged Laurel standing between two large, black Dobermans.

"Wow."

"When Laurel was a teenager, she loved helping her father train them." Helene's eyes softened. "They would do almost anything she asked them to. As long as there was a treat for them in store." She looked up. "I know they look fierce, but they were sweet animals."

"Were?" Cash asked.

"Well, these particular dogs are no longer with us."

"They're dead?" His tone was abrupt.

She pointed at the picture. "Apollo passed five years ago, and then Nina last year."

Maya raised a brow at Cash. Why was he asking about their dogs?

"Do you have any others?" he asked.

"Yes, Wade keeps a few for breeding and sells the puppies." She looked at Maya. "It's only a hobby. He doesn't show them anymore, but I think it reminds him of the times he and Laurel spent together."

"Are they here?" Cash asked.

"No, we don't have room for them in the suburbs. They stay at our home in Greenley."

The city of Greenley was a rural, mountainous town north of Pendleton. Lots of big farms owned for generations and some kept by the wealthy looking for a place to get away from the city.

"We have a nice kennel and outdoor lots for them," Helene said. "An older couple lives on the grounds and takes care of the feeding." She looked at Cash. "Why do you ask?"

Maya wondered the same thing.

But Cash only shrugged. "Just curious." He looked at Maya. "We should get going."

Helene rose, as did Maya, and followed them to the foyer.

"Oh, do you mind giving me your number again?" Maya asked. "I…lost it."

She hadn't told Helene about being pushed into the lake. No reason to give the woman more to worry about than she already had.

Helene recited her number, and Maya programmed it into her new phone. "Thanks." She squeezed the woman's hand.

"We'll be in touch." Cash opened the door and hurried back to his sedan.

"What was that all about?" Maya asked as soon as they were back in the vehicle. "Why all the questions about the dogs? And are you feeling all right?" She pressed a hand to his arm. "You remembered something, didn't you?"

He nodded.

"That's great, Cash."

"No, it's not." He turned to her. "We need to pay a visit to Wade DeWitt."

Wade DeWitt's office was in a high-rise building in downtown Atlanta. Cash had explained his recovered memory and his theory on the short drive from the DeWitts' home in Orchard Park.

"Okay," Maya said, trying to put the pieces together. "You think Wade DeWitt sicced his dog on you somewhere in the Pendleton industrial park?"

"I think a Doberman chased me. And Wade owns Dobermans. On a farm in Greenley, which is a half hour north of Pendleton." He speared her with his gaze as they stopped at a crosswalk while a group of pedestrians crossed the street.

She had to admit, it all added up to more than a coincidence. But did she think Laurel's father could be somehow linked to her disappearance? The man was vain. Pompous. Too concerned with his reputation and business dealings. But would he do something to harm his own daughter?

Maya didn't want to believe that was possible. Wade was the only father Laurel had ever known. And Maya wanted her sister to have the family she'd never had. Parents who loved her and took care of her.

"And you're sure this memory was from that night in Pendleton? Not some other time?" she asked.

Cash sighed as he slowly passed the office building. "There's no street parking available. I'm going to have to try the parking deck across from the building." He took a right and pulled up to the gate, waiting for the machine to spit out a ticket.

"You don't like parking decks?"

He pulled inside and began searching for an empty spot. "No. As a general rule, they're hard to get in and out of quickly. Not ideal if you need to leave in a hurry."

He drove up the ramp to the second level and found an empty spot near the middle of the outward row. Putting the sedan in Park, he turned off the ignition and faced her. "And yes, I think the memory was from that night. I've never been chased by a Doberman before."

She couldn't argue with that.

They exited the car and walked to the elevator, reached the first floor, and then crossed the street to Wade's building. The sign on the wall of the marbled lobby said DeWitt Enterprises was on the seventeenth floor of the twenty-story building.

They entered the elevator, and Cash punched the button for seventeen.

"So, are we hot or cold?" she asked.

"What?" Cash's eyebrows rose.

Heat flushed her cheeks. "For the interrogation," she said, trying to backtrack. "You know, are we going in hot? Or the other way?"

"Oh." He pressed his lips. "Well, he already knows you're working with the GBI, right?"

"Yes, although he made it clear he wanted the investigation to stay out of the media."

Cash nodded. "Seems like controlling the narrative is important for him. If we take that away, he'll likely shut down. Lawyer up. Probably best to keep it casual."

"Got it. And his assistant?"

"Since you've met her before, let's build on that. You take the lead."

The elevator dinged, and the doors opened to a well-appointed reception area. Plush beige carpeting led to a curved reception desk.

Maya recognized the assistant from the DeWitts' home. Audra. She looked up as they approached. Her eyes widened slightly. "May I help you?"

"Yes, Miss…" Maya glanced at the name plate. "Peterson, hello. Maya Reid. We met at the DeWitts' home last week."

"I remember. Nice to see you again." Her tone was pleasant, but the sentiment didn't quite reach her eyes.

"And this is Special Agent Cash Brenner of the GBI," Maya said. "We'd like to speak to Mr. DeWitt, please."

Audra cut her eyes to Cash, then back to Maya. "Mr. DeWitt is in a meeting."

"We can wait," Cash said.

"I'm afraid he's booked solid for the rest of the afternoon."

Maya glanced at Cash briefly, then smiled at the assistant. "I understand he's a busy man, but this is regarding his daughter. We won't keep him long, but we do have important information we need to share."

"Perhaps you could come back tomorrow. Or speak with Mrs. DeWitt."

"Perhaps," Cash said, leaning an elbow on the tall counter, "you could squeeze us in between appointments." He smiled, laying on the charm.

The woman's eyes narrowed slightly. She didn't seem affected by Cash's allure. Instead, she pursed her lips and leaned in slightly. "I'm sorry. Mr. DeWitt is unavailable." Her tone was cold, words clipped and short.

A muscle in Cash's jaw jumped and his fingers twitched.

The two stared at each other as the power struggle played out.

"Did it just get hot in here?" Maya asked.

Cash nodded, then headed for the walnut double doors beyond the reception area. Maya followed as Audra jumped up from her chair and scrambled after them. Her calls to stop went unheeded as Cash reached the doors and stormed in.

NINE

Wade DeWitt sat behind his heavy wooden desk wearing a headset with a microphone attached. He was flipping through a folder in his hands but turned as they entered. His startled gaze bounced from Cash to Maya to his assistant behind them.

"What is the meaning of this?" He dropped the folder onto the desk.

Cash held up his badge. "Special Agent Brenner, GBI. I need to ask you a few questions regarding your daughter, Laurel DeWitt."

Wade's eyes grew large, then narrowed. "Robert, I'll call you back." He clicked off the headset, then flung it onto his desk. "You can't come barging into this office, waving a badge—"

"I assure you, I can," Cash said.

"Should I call security, sir?" Miss Peterson askcd.

Hands on hips, Wade measured Cash with his gaze.

Cash stood his ground, daring the man to defy him.

Wade blinked, then sighed. "No, it's fine, Audra. Give us a few minutes, please."

She nodded and retreated, closing the doors behind her.

"Have you found her?" Wade's voice held a mixture of hope and fear.

Maybe he did care about his daughter after all.

"No," Maya answered. "Not yet."

His shoulders slumped.

"The GBI is continuing to explore a number of avenues," Cash said. "But you should know that Dillon Cordell was killed this afternoon."

"He…what?" Wade sat back in his chair.

Genuine surprise lit his expression.

Maybe Maya was right, and Wade didn't have anything to do with Laurel's disappearance. Cash hoped it was true.

"May I ask what happened?" Wade said.

"He was killed in a car…accident," Cash said. Wade would learn soon enough that the car had exploded. The media had already started swarming the scene when they left. "Mr. DeWitt, do you own a Doberman pinscher?"

Wade blinked at the sudden change in subject. "Yes. Well, actually, the breed I own is the European Doberman. The term pinscher is only applied to the American breed."

"But you do own the dog?" Cash wasn't in the mood to debate the finer points of breed terminology.

"A number of them."

"And where were you on March 14?"

"I…" Wade clicked a couple of keys on his computer. "I was at a business dinner."

"Can anyone confirm that?"

"Yes. We had reservations for six at San Martell's. You can check with the maître d'."

He'd get Addie or Owen on it as soon as they left the building. "And what time did you leave the meeting?"

"Oh, I'd say…nine. Maybe nine fifteen. Why?"

"Where did you go afterwards?"

"Home. You can also confirm that with my wife and our housekeeper."

Both of whom would have good reasons to cover for him if he weren't telling the truth. "Is there security footage from that night we could see?"

"We use a service for that. But I don't understand the relevancy of—"

"I'd like the name of that service, please."

Wade crossed his arms. "Miss Peterson can get you the name and number on your way out."

He was pushing Wade's patience, but he had to keep the upper hand, perhaps cause the man to make a mistake if he kept to rapid-firing questions. "I'll do that. And where are your dogs now?"

"At our mountain home in Greenley. We have a large kennel there."

"And when was the last time you were at this property?"

"A couple of months ago."

"Is that normal for you to go so long without seeing your dogs?"

"I've been busy with an important business deal. And then we had a trip to Italy. Otherwise, I try to get out there once a month or so." His eyes narrowed. "If you are accusing me of something, I'd like to know what it is."

Cash had questioned enough suspects to tell when one was about to shut down. And Wade DeWitt was getting close. "I'm simply asking to confirm your whereabouts on a specific date. Any way we could visit your property, take a look at those dogs?"

"Why would you need to do that?"

"It's pertinent to our investigation. And that's all I need to tell you."

"Then you'll need to speak with my attorney from here on out." Wade rounded the desk, heading for the door. He opened it and waited for them to exit.

He was done, but Cash had one more card to play. "We could also come back with a search warrant."

Wade clenched his jaw. "Be my guest."

Cash glanced at Maya and nodded. Time to make their exit.

They headed out the door to Miss Peterson's desk. "I'd like the name and number for the security service at Mr. DeWitt's home."

She opened her mouth, but Wade cut her off. "Just give it to them, Audra." With one final glare at Cash, he slammed his office door.

Tightlipped, Audra tapped her keyboard, then handed Cash the paper from the printer.

He checked the page. Sentinel Home Systems had a good reputation. It shouldn't be hard to check with them to confirm DeWitt's alibi.

"Have a nice day." He tipped a finger to his forehead and followed Maya to the elevator.

As the doors closed, he caught a final look at Miss Peterson.

"I'd like to wipe that smug look off her face," Maya said.

No doubt she could do it, too. He might pay good money to see that.

They exited the building and crossed the street.

"What now?" she asked.

"Now we get a search warrant for the security footage from the DeWitts' home and the kennel."

Maya's brows pulled together as they got on the elevator in the parking deck. "You think Wade left a business meeting, drove to Greenley, picked up a dog, went to the industrial park in Pendleton and unleashed the dog on you?"

"Even if he left the meeting at nine thirty p.m., then according to when that call came in and I went to the industrial park, he would've had time."

"But how would he know you would be there?"

"I don't know, but getting the footage is step one."

They reached the second floor and headed for Cash's sedan.

"Why?" he asked. "You think I'm completely off base on this?"

She stopped at her side of the car and shook her head. "No,

I see the merits of your theory. But… I don't want it to be true. Her own father?"

They'd both seen enough of human nature to know that people were capable of evil. But he could understand why Maya would want to believe that her sister's adoptive father—the only father figure she'd ever had—would only shower his daughter with love.

And he was stripping that away. Piece by piece.

He propped a hand on the roof of the car, holding his keys ready. "Look," he said. "I could be totally wrong here—"

The window of the car next to her shattered.

Maya screamed and dropped out of sight. Cash raced around the car to her side.

A bullet? He hadn't heard a gunshot. And no way to tell where the shooter was.

"Are you hit?"

She lay on the ground, glass shards strewn around her. "No." Her voice was muffled as she tucked her head under her arms.

"Come on." He reached for her hand. "Let's take cover."

She grabbed his hand and started to stand.

A red dot appeared on her chest. The sniper had her in his sights.

"No!" He yelled, pulling her down and leaning over her.

Something slammed into him, knocking him on his back. Searing pain burned through his right shoulder.

He'd been shot.

"Cash!" Fear ripped through Maya as Cash's grip on her was pulled away. She opened her eyes to see him on the ground, red flowing from his shoulder.

"I'm okay." He grunted, his face contorted with pain.

Crawling over the glass on the pavement, he crouched next to her as she used the cement half-wall of the parking deck as a shield.

No more shots rang around them, which must mean they were hidden from the shooter's point of view.

"Let me see." Gently pulling back his shirt collar, she checked the wound. Two holes, one in front and one in back. "It went all the way through." Which was better than the bullet being lodged in his shoulder.

She pressed a hand on either side of the wound to staunch the bleeding.

"I'll call it in." While he called dispatch, she took a few deep breaths. Adrenaline coursed through her, sending small tremors through her hands.

Cash had pushed her down, covered her with his body. Taken a bullet meant for her.

Just doing his job, right?

She risked a glance at him.

His face was pale. Small beads of sweat peppered his brow.

He had to be hurting, but he spoke calmly and concisely on the phone.

"Atlanta PD should be here any minute," he said, clicking off the call. "Owen and Addie are on their way."

"Are they still in Dansby?" That was over a half hour away.

"Actually, they were on the way to the Atlanta lab, so they're about ten minutes out."

"What do we do in the meantime?"

"Sit tight. Try not to get shot." He attempted a smile. "At least, not again."

"Cash, I—" She swallowed the emotions rising in her chest. "Thank you."

His gaze shifted to hers, the intensity in his eyes stealing her breath and holding her captive.

She was aware of her hands pressed to his shoulder. His nearness. Her heart thudded and her fingers shook as his eyes dropped to her lips. He leaned closer. So close she could feel his breath on her cheek.

Sirens split the air as a couple of Atlanta Police Department cruisers pulled up, followed by an ambulance. Everything moved in a blur as officers surrounded them, getting them to safety. Then the paramedics took over, putting Cash in the back of their vehicle to address his wound.

Someone handed her wipes, and she rubbed Cash's blood off her hands as she gave her statement to the APD detective on the scene. But she kept watch on Cash in the back of the ambulance as the paramedics worked on him. He nodded in answer to their questions, but his gaze tracked back to her.

Every time their eyes met, butterflies danced in her stomach. Could she be falling for Cash again? No. She could never let that happen. Promised herself it wouldn't. Not ever. Being on this case, saving each other's lives. It was messing with her emotions. At least, that's what she told herself.

Addie and Owen arrived, followed by SAC Overstreet. She filled them in on the events as well as their conversation with Wade DeWitt.

Overstreet rubbed his chin. "And you two came here to question DeWitt because Cash remembered something from the night of his accident?"

"Yes." She briefly explained the memory Cash had recalled at the DeWitt home.

"And Cash remembered the attack because he saw a picture of Laurel with Dobermans?" Owen asked.

"Apparently. The dogs look similar to the one he said chased him, and it must've triggered the memory."

"There's more." Cash stepped into their small group huddle.

"Shouldn't you be headed for the hospital?" Addie raised her brows.

Cash shook his head. "It's not that bad. Clean shot, straight through. Didn't hit anything major. Paramedics fixed me up and gave me the all-clear."

Maya stared at him. How was he standing there like everything was normal? "Are you sure—"

Overstreet raised his hand, cutting off Maya's protest. "Save your breath." He turned to Cash. "I know better than to argue with you, Brenner. But you said there was more?"

"Right." Cash's brows pulled together. "I remembered something else. When the first bullet hit the window behind you, Maya, the glass went everywhere."

She had pieces of it in her hair, on her clothes. "That triggered another memory?"

"Yeah. I…jumped through a window."

"You what?" Addie's mouth gaped open.

Maya felt hers doing the same. They all turned to Cash.

"When was this?" Owen asked.

"I think it was the same night as the dog attack." His eyes focused on something far off. "I could hear the dog barking. I was running. Panicked. No other choice. No way out. And then I jumped through a window. Fell. Landed hard." He refocused on them. "I think that's how I dislocated my shoulder."

"Not when you crashed into the tree?" Maya's mind went back to the scene. Cash's car had been crumpled, mangled metal. Cuts, slivers of glass everywhere. His shoulder hanging at that odd angle.

She'd assumed everything had happened as a result of the car accident. But it was possible he was injured before. Which would explain why he'd been driving so erratically and almost hit her.

"It would make sense," he said, confirming her own thoughts. "If I were injured, I wouldn't have been able to drive very well."

Overstreet nodded to Addie. "Get ASAC Hasler on the phone. Tell him to send Watts and Chandler back to the industrial park. I know we've surveyed there already but have them look for a building with a broken window. Or one that has been recently repaired. Check with the businesses to see if anyone remembers a window repair in the last two weeks."

Addie stepped away to make the call.

"Thank you, sir." Cash said to Overstreet.

"For what?"

"For believing my story. My weird and scattered memories."

Overstreet nodded. "I had a feeling that working with Miss Reid would jog your brain. Knock some of that stuff loose." He tipped his head toward her.

He was right. Working together had knocked loose some of Cash's memories, hopefully aiding their investigation. It had also knocked loose her buried feelings. Something that would benefit no one.

She glanced away as Cash's gaze fell on her again.

"Sir," Cash said. "Given this new information, should we have another chat with Mr. DeWitt?"

"I'd say that's a good idea. Let me get the all clear." He stepped over to speak to the APD detective.

"What do you say?" Cash asked Maya, standing close enough for his cologne to flood her senses. "You up for another meeting with Wade?"

She steeled her features. "Of course." Whatever it took to get her sister back.

The sooner they found Laurel, the better it would be. For everyone.

The elevator in Wade's building was tight quarters, with Cash wedged between SAC Overstreet and Owen. Addie and Maya were tucked behind them, and in front, Detective Vincent and a couple APD officers. This was APD's jurisdiction, and as the first on the scene, they were in charge.

Cash's shoulder throbbed, but the pain reliever from the paramedics took the ache down to about a five, at least. Maya shifted behind him, the vanilla scent of her shampoo wafting over him. He'd known fear. Especially over the past few days. When he'd seen her car go over the bridge. When he'd found her on the floor of her home, unconscious.

But seeing that red dot on her chest, knowing a sniper's bullet was about to end her life... He'd never known fear like that.

Yes, it was his job to protect. But it was more than a sense of duty that had motivated him. Pushed him into action to cover her before the bullet found her.

It couldn't be love. He wouldn't even entertain the thought. He couldn't love Maya Reid. Or anyone. The ramifications, the risks, were too high.

He'd wanted to kiss her. Almost had. Right there on the second level of the parking deck. Hiding from a shooter. Adrenaline and emotions from being shot had been pumping through his system, clouding his judgment.

That was a mistake he wouldn't make again.

He had to find a way to put her back in the box labeled "professional working relationship only." To create some space between them and find his footing again.

The alternative was too dangerous. For both of them.

They reached the seventeenth floor, and the elevator dinged as the doors opened to the DeWitt Enterprises reception area. The group exited and descended on Miss Peterson en masse.

She stood as she took in the group of law enforcement officers.

Detective Vincent flashed his badge. "We'd like to speak to Mr. DeWitt, please."

"H-he's not here."

"Where is he?" Vincent asked.

"He's gone." She found Cash in the group, her eyes meeting his. "After you and Miss Reid left, he said he had an appointment."

Cash glanced at the closed door to Wade's office. He could be hiding in there. "Mind if we check?"

"Go ahead."

He and the APD officers entered the room, but it was empty. With no exits inside. He returned to the reception area. "All clear."

Vincent nodded, then turned back to Miss Peterson. "When did he leave?"

She checked her watch. "Maybe a half hour ago?"

That tracked with the timeline for when he and Maya entered the parking deck, shots were fired at them, and then the emergency personnel showed up and secured the scene.

"Did he say where he was going?" Vincent asked.

"No. He said an appointment. Then he got on the elevator and left."

"Where would his car be parked?"

"There's a small employee parking lot behind the building. But I think he had a car service drop him off today. He does that sometimes instead of driving in."

"I'm going to need the name of that service. And we're going to need to see the security footage from the building."

"Of course." Miss Peterson tapped on her keyboard. She wrote down the name of the service on a card and handed it to Detective Vincent. "The cameras for our floor are separate from the main building. I can pull up our surveillance feed from here."

"Give us the last half hour."

Cash joined Vincent and Overstreet at the monitor. The footage rolled, showing Cash and Maya's arrival and exit.

"No sound?" Cash asked.

Miss Peterson shook her head. Then Wade came into the reception area. He and Miss Peterson exchanged a few words, then she stood from the desk.

The screen blipped, then showed gray.

"What happened?"

"I don't know." She clicked the keys again, backed up the

recording. But the feed went blank at the same time. "I'm so sorry. I don't know what's wrong."

Overstreet nodded to Vincent. "Let's go to the lobby and get the building's footage."

Ten minutes later, the group was crowded into the main security team's office, checking the cameras for the lobby. Wade DeWitt did not get off the elevator on the first floor. Nor did any of the exterior cameras show him exiting the building.

Where had he gone?

"Is there any other way to leave this building?" Vincent asked.

"There's a lower level," the security team leader said. "Only mechanical stuff down there. And one door that opens to the alley for deliveries."

"Let's go."

Cash's nerves hitched, the pain in his shoulder a reminder of the danger.

The group headed for the stairs leading to the lower level. Cash reached a hand for Maya. "Stay here."

"What?"

"We don't know what's waiting for us down there. What state Wade may be in. Or if he's armed."

"Which means you need all the help you can get."

"Yeah. From trained law enforcement officers."

She narrowed her eyes. "But I—"

"I know. You're a PI. But that's not the same." He held her gaze, willing her to understand. He couldn't risk her getting hurt again. "Please, Maya. I need you to stay here. Preferably in the security office."

Where she would be guarded by guys with guns.

She let out a sigh. "Fine. But you come get me the minute you find him."

"Promise."

Cash headed down the stairs with the rest of the group. Guns drawn, they entered the darkened area in single file, then spread out to clear the area. His shoulder burned, but thankfully the bullet had hit his right side. His left arm, although still sore from the dislocated shoulder, was solid.

With Owen on his wing, Cash made his way systematically through the space. The lower level of the building was divided by support walls and beams, with air and heating equipment scattered throughout.

The darkness of the room felt like a thick coat that lay over him. His pulse picked up and sweat broke out on his forehead. A slight tremor flowed through his hands.

Images flashed in his mind, interspersing with the present. Darkness. Empty rooms. Searching. For…what? He willed his muddled brain to make sense of it all.

He'd been in an area similar to this. Alone. Gun in hand. And then running. Being chased. The dog. The window. Pain.

He stumbled.

"Cash?" Owen's quiet voice reached him. "You okay, man?"

"I…" His breath came in gasps.

Shouts of "all clear" came from around the space as the other officers sounded off.

"Clear," Owen called and dropped his weapon. He pulled Cash to the hallway.

Cash dropped to the bottom step.

"You remembered something else, didn't you?" Owen asked.

"Yeah." He explained the memories. If only he could remember where he'd been and why.

But there was something else. Something just beyond his grasp. Another memory he had yet to recover. He wanted desperately to remember. And yet, he knew that when he did, it would change everything.

The door opened as the rest of the team entered and headed up the stairs. Cash stood and followed, ignoring the questioning looks from the other team members.

The dread of having to face Maya curled in his gut. He didn't want to have to tell her that they were empty-handed. But it was the truth.

Wade DeWitt was not in the building.

But where had he gone? Innocent people didn't hide. Or disappear.

Wade was in the wind.

And so was the possibility of finding him.

The conference room at the GBI office looked like a tornado had hit. Files and paperwork were scattered among the laptops being used by members of the Bravo team, who'd converged here yesterday after Wade's disappearance.

SAC Overstreet commanded the room like a conductor, managing the various personnel as everyone went over the evidence and case files. A whiteboard on the wall as well as maps and other charts held varying degrees of brainstorming and known facts.

Tucked into a corner, Maya watched the controlled chaos. Again, it struck her how different it was to work with a team. And what she might have been missing by choosing to work solo.

There may have been a number of things she'd missed out on in life by building walls around her heart to keep others out. But it had been the only way she knew to keep herself safe.

There was a statewide BOLO issued for Wade DeWitt, who was now a person of interest in Laurel's disappearance. But since he'd left his office yesterday, no sightings had been reported. The car service claimed they'd dropped him off at the building that morning, but no call had come to pick him up. He had simply vanished.

Maya had checked in with Helene a few times. The woman was beside herself with worry. Her sister and brother-in-law had flown in from Florida to stay with her, and a couple Atlanta PD officers were sitting on the house in case Wade returned or attempted to make contact.

She wanted badly to comfort Helene. To tell her they were wrong, and that Wade wasn't involved, but all signs were pointing otherwise.

The sheriff's office in Greenley had also been sent to the DeWitts' mountain home and kennel, but no signs of Wade there either. This morning, the GBI had been granted a warrant for all of Wade's financials. Cash's team was scouring the information on his properties and holdings, looking for anything that would point to where Wade could be.

Helene had given them any info she had, and there was a freeze on Wade's credit cards and bank accounts. If he tried to leave the country, they would know.

Addie stood from the computer she'd been working on and stepped over to the table near Maya, pouring herself a fresh cup of coffee.

"How you doing?" Maya asked.

Addie rubbed her eyes and suppressed a yawn. "Could've used a few more winks, but I'll make it."

The agents had worked into the night, first physically searching for Wade, and then switching to a virtual search. Maya had stayed with the team, but since Wade's disappearance had become an official investigation, she was only allowed to observe and answer questions as needed.

"How about you?" Addie tipped her head.

"I'm fine." She'd finally gotten access to her house last night after her landlord had a new door installed and the forensics team had cleared out. Addie had gone with her while she grabbed a change of clothes and her laptop, which she used to look for any information that might help find Wade.

"You and Cash have been through a lot the last few days." Addie gave her a light squeeze on the arm, then returned to her work.

Maya let her gaze rest on Cash across the room. He talked with Overstreet, checking points off on the map.

Since they had left Wade's building and returned to the GBI office yesterday, things between them had felt different. With the entire team working together, there'd been no time for them to be alone together. And no need.

She was protected in the office, surrounded by agents. Cash was no longer her partner on Laurel's case. His focus had shifted to the job at hand and not on her.

As it should be.

Working with the GBI was still her best chance at finding her sister, but her partnership had only been temporary. With most of Cash's memories returned and the investigation centered on Wade, there was no reason for him to be at her side.

He'd barely spoken a handful of words to her all morning. But what did she expect?

There had been a moment between them as she'd held his wounds. Or at least she'd thought so. In the heat of the moment, emotions had run high. Cash had been shot. Wounded. And she'd almost been killed. It would be easy to misunderstand feelings for something more.

Wasn't that what she'd done before? Misinterpreted his behavior to think she'd meant more to him than she had?

And that had only led to heartbreak.

She wouldn't go down that road with Cash again. Couldn't.

Best to follow his lead and keep things professional. Distant. Safe.

Focusing on her laptop, she dug deeper into DeWitt Enterprises, searching for a clue. Her only task right now was finding Wade. And her sister.

Nothing else mattered. Certainly not any feelings she may have for Cash Brenner.

She'd looked into the dog breeding that Wade did. His animals were certainly top quality and had numerous awards to prove it. The DeWitt Dobermans were well known in the show world. But everything seemed aboveboard. Nothing that would indicate a crime.

There had to be something else they were missing.

Her mind went back to the industrial park. The nexus of her case and Cash's. Laurel had most definitely been there to take the picture she'd posted on her social media. And Cash had been there for a reason that was still unknown.

But could anything link to Wade? Only one way to find out.

Half an hour later, she sat back from the computer. "Huh."

"What's that?" Owen asked. He'd stepped to the table to get a bottle of water and a chocolate chip muffin. He leaned over her shoulder, looking at the laptop. "You find something?"

"I don't know. Maybe."

Owen asked SAC Overstreet to join them. Cash came with him, and the rest of the eyes in the room turned toward her.

Heat flushed her cheeks. If she were wrong and this was nothing, she'd feel foolish. One of the many reasons she worked alone.

"What've you got, Miss Reid?" Overstreet said.

She explained. "So, I dug into the various businesses that have buildings around the industrial park. Most are owned by well-known companies. A few smaller ones. But none that seem to have a connection to Wade or DeWitt Enterprises. And then there are a few which are older. On the east side of the park."

"The original land," Cash said. "The west side is the new expansion."

"Right. And some of these buildings are so old they aren't being used any more. So, I looked into them to see who owned them. And I found this." She turned her laptop around to show one of the buildings she'd researched.

"What about it?" Overstreet asked.

"It's owned by a company called Nyne Lyves, spelled with *y*'s instead of *i*'s."

"What is that?" Cash asked. "A cat food company?"

"You'd think. But it doesn't seem to actually exist. The web address goes to a page that says the site's under construction. I can't find an owner or any kind of board of directors. And no listing with the Better Business Bureau. But there's more."

She tapped the keyboard to bring up the aerial map of the land. "There's another building behind this one, not listed with an address, but definitely part of the same property."

Cash leaned closer to see, and his face paled. He blinked a few times, beads of sweat breaking out on his forehead.

"Brenner?" Overstreet said, placing a hand on his shoulder. "You okay?"

"I… I remember that building. Something…" He rubbed his palms over his eyes. "Something there. I—" His eyes shot to Maya, then he averted his gaze. "Sir?" He turned back to Overstreet. "Can we talk in your office?"

What was that look? It reminded her of when her foster parents had to tell her that she would be moving again.

Overstreet touched her shoulder. "Good work, Miss Reid. Agent Chandler, see what you can find out about this company."

"On it, sir." Chandler began tapping keys on his keyboard.

If there was anything to find about Nyne Lyves, Noah could find it. His reputation in the cyber forensics area was formidable.

Cash made a beeline for the door. Whatever he remembered had him upset. She wished for a moment that it was just the two of them again, so he would share with her. Temporary or not, she had enjoyed being a team with Cash. But now she got the idea he was shutting her out. And it gave her a bad feeling.

TEN

While the rest of the team went into action, obtaining a search warrant and gathering what was needed for a raid on the warehouse, Maya slipped out of the conference room. She headed down the hall toward the SAC's office. Was she about to eavesdrop on a GBI agent and his boss? Maybe. It was probably a bad idea, but she couldn't shake the feeling that whatever they were discussing had to do with her. And she was desperate enough to do something dumb.

A door shut, and voices carried down the hall. Cash's voice. He was coming her way. Maya rerouted toward the break room as Cash rounded the corner. He stopped when he saw her, eyes widening slightly.

"Hi," she said, hoping her voice sounded as nonchalant as she intended. "I was going to grab a snack. Want anything?"

He tilted his head, those piercing blue eyes holding a question.

"Addie said there were some organic nut bars in the cabinet." She shrugged. "I need protein before the raid."

Something she couldn't read crossed his expression, then he motioned for her to enter the room ahead of him.

The break room was empty, the hum of vending machines the only sound.

He regarded her but didn't speak.

A sense of foreboding trickled up her spine.

"What, Cash? Just say it."

"You're not coming on the raid."

Her mind whirled. "Are you serious? Why not?"

"This is a GBI investigation."

"I understand that, but I'm still part of this case and—"

"We don't know what we might…find at the warehouse."

"This is the same building you were in when you got hurt, right?"

"Yes, but I don't remember everything about that night. It could be dangerous."

"I can stay in the car."

He raised a brow. "I've heard that before."

"I promise this time. I mean it."

Cash shook his head. "The risks are too high. We can't afford to take a civilian."

"A civil—" She crossed her arms. "I'm hardly that."

"You aren't law enforcement, Maya."

It was true. She couldn't argue with the truth. But she thought she'd more than proved herself a capable ally. Worthy. Someone who could hold her own and be a valuable part of the team.

Heart sinking, she looked for another tactic. "Maybe if I talked to Overstreet, I could—"

He held up a hand. "The decision was mine." His expression was stone. Unyielding.

The ground under her feet shifted.

That was it. It wasn't that Overstreet didn't think she could handle it.

Cash didn't want her.

On the team.

Or otherwise.

Just like every time she had hoped a foster family might keep her. But then she would be sent elsewhere.

Just like it had felt when Cash had broken up with her two years ago.

Unwanted.

She backed away, retreating behind her wall again. She never should have ventured out of it in the first place.

"You can wait here at the station, if you'd like. Or, I can have someone take you home."

After the incident with the drug overdose, her home no longer felt like the safe haven it once had been. Her worry wouldn't be lessened there. No, she needed to be as close to the action as possible. And the station was as close as Cash was going to let her get.

"I'll wait here."

"Fine. I'll brief you once we return."

"Understood." Her words tasted as hard and bitter as they sounded.

Cash gave a tight nod and walked away, leaving her alone in the room.

Hot tears burned her eyes, but she refused to let them fall. She stepped into the restroom, splashing some cold water on her face and getting her emotions under control before returning to the conference room.

The team continued to prepare for the raid. Maya found her corner again but no longer felt like a part of the group. Now she observed only as an outsider.

Once the search warrant was granted, the team filed out of the room. Maya watched them go, feeling for all the world like the same little girl who stood by as others left without her.

She pushed the emotions aside. Cash had remembered something important about the warehouse, and he didn't want her there. What were they walking into?

Cash slammed his locker door a little too hard. Owen raised an eyebrow at him but said nothing. Good, because the last thing Cash wanted to do was to rehash the conversation with

Maya. Telling her to stay behind was the right thing to do, but that didn't mean it had been easy. Or even what he'd wanted.

Which made him angry at himself all over again. He shoved into his tactical vest and checked his weapons while hot emotion roiled through him.

These past few days with Maya…being her partner, working with her, trusting her…had opened up places in his heart he thought were long buried.

But they needed to be locked away once more.

He couldn't afford to get involved with Maya Reid. For both their sakes. Two hearts broken was too high a price to pay. And he'd promised himself he wouldn't hurt her again.

Except he had. The pain had flickered in her eyes before she'd shuttered the door on her emotions. He knew that move. Had perfected it for years.

Cash wiped a hand down his face as if to remove the thoughts and feelings churning inside him. He had a job to do, and he couldn't afford to lose focus.

Following Owen to their vehicle, he climbed into the passenger side. The scenery flew past as they drove to the industrial park in Pendleton, but Cash could only see one thing. The warehouse.

It had all come rushing back to him like a dam breaking, flooding his mind with memories.

He'd gone to that old, abandoned warehouse, the one Maya had pulled up on her computer, because the voice on the call had told him he would find answers about Elizabeth. One of his more impulsive moves. A calculated risk, he liked to believe. But the truth was, his desperation had overcome good sense. And his training. He'd rushed to the warehouse and gone in half-cocked.

And it had almost cost him his life.

It may have cost the lives of others, too.

How many more young women had been hurt in the time it

had taken him to remember? Dansby PD had yet to find Kellie Ryles, the young woman they'd confirmed had left the club with Cordell. Her life lay squarely on Cash's shoulders.

Owen pulled into the parking lot of a business in the industrial park. Per procedure, they were setting up in an adjacent area and would go into the warehouse in stealth mode. Stopping the vehicle behind Overstreet's SUV, he turned off the ignition.

"So," Owen said. "Are you going to tell me what has you wound tighter than a drum?"

Cash flicked a glance at his partner, unsure where to start.

"What are we going to find in the warehouse? What did you remember?"

"It's still fuzzy, but there were rooms. More like cells. A handful of them."

"Cells? As in jail?"

He clenched his jaw. "Holding pens."

Owen's eyebrows raised. "Trafficking?"

"Likely."

"Terrible." He blew out a breath. "How did Maya take it? And why isn't she here?"

"I didn't tell her. And I asked Overstreet to exclude her."

"Why?"

"Because...she's not law enforcement. Not a trained officer."

"Yeah, I know. But so far, she's been able to hold up her end."

Cash shook his head. "This isn't the same. It's too...dangerous."

"You care about her."

It wasn't a question.

No use denying it. His partner knew him too well.

"And the other reason?" Owen asked.

"What?"

"Why didn't you tell her what you'd remembered?"

The memory hit him like a punch. A gold necklace with the letter *L*.

"There was a body in there. It might be Laurel."

Owen's sigh echoed his own. "And you didn't want to tell Maya until you knew for sure."

"No need to devastate her if it's not her sister."

"Right."

They exited the car and joined the rest of the team for Overstreet's final orders, then Cash led the way to the warehouse.

Memories of that night came to him like flashes of lightning in a summer thunderstorm. Round after round, he remembered walking up to the building and entering the dark interior. Stepping through the empty space. Looking for something, anything, to lead him to Elizabeth.

And then, finding the small rooms, side by side, with iron bars and locks on the doors.

Behind him, the quiet footsteps of his team followed him to the area, then spread out. Radios clicked as officers cleared the building, finding no one.

Not even the dog.

The smell of bleach permeated the air.

Whoever had been using this building had wiped it clean. Probably moved their operation to another location. And likely the body.

And they'd had plenty of time to do so since Cash hadn't been able to lead anyone back here.

Once again, he blasted himself for not being able to remember.

"Why not burn the place down?" Watts asked.

"That would bring the fire department," Cash guessed. "Place too much attention on the building and the owner."

Overstreet approached, repeating what Cash had already concluded. "Agent King, get your forensics unit down here. Have them scour the place. Bleached or not, there's got to be something they left behind. A hair, fiber, a fingerprint. I want this place scrubbed."

Cash prayed they found something that might link them to whoever had been here.

Perpetrator or victim.

Defeat lay over him like a hot blanket.

"Wait," Owen said. "The body. Was it here, in one of these rooms?"

Cash closed his eyes, mentally walking through his steps that night. His head shot up. "No. It was… I found the cells first. No one was here. Then, I went this way."

He turned, heading for the far end of the building. Down the back staircase. To the basement. Memories grew thicker, as did the darkness. He flicked on his flashlight at the bottom of the stairs.

The lower level was a mess, with trash and debris scattered across the dirt floor. A dark stain ran along the wall about three feet high.

"Water line," Owen said from behind him.

"The basement had flooded recently. I remember the ground being damp, and the musty smell was still strong." Cash led them further into the large space, and then around the corner. Near the furnace, he stopped. "She was here."

"Who?" Overstreet asked.

He'd thought it might be Laurel, but it couldn't have been her. Maya's sister had only been missing for a few weeks, but what he'd found hadn't been a corpse. He had remembered it wrong. The memory came back clearer than before. "Nothing left but a skeleton." His stomach threatened to rebel as he recalled the discovery.

"How do you know it was a she?" Addie's voice was quiet behind him.

"The bones were small, petite. Female. Probably buried down here a few years ago. I think the flooding loosened the grave, uncovered the bones."

"Did you see anything else?"

"A gold necklace. Near the skull. Probably had been around her neck."

The SAC commanded the team to begin searching the room for any signs of the remains.

"They won't find her," Cash said to Owen. "Whoever did this knows I found the bones. That's when they chased me out of the building. And they've had plenty of time to come back, remove the skeleton and clean up any evidence."

"There could be something they missed. There usually is." Owen clapped a hand on his shoulder. "Don't give up hope yet."

"I found it!" Addie called.

Cash rushed forward, his flashlight shining on the object in Addie's gloved hand.

The necklace.

"It was over in the corner under some debris." She dropped it into Cash's palm, and he turned it over in his hand.

Now that he held it, he could see clearly. Not an *L*, as he'd feared. The top and middle sections had broken off. It was an *E*.

Elizabeth.

Maya was on her third cup of tea, but she had switched to decaf. Her nerves didn't need any more momentum. They were jumping along her spine all on their own.

How long did it take to check out an empty building?

It felt like an eternity, but in reality, it had only been an hour and a half since Cash and the rest of his team had left the GBI office. Driving to the Pendleton industrial park would take a half hour, and then there would be prep to storm the building and, depending on what they found, time to thoroughly check everything.

She had moved from the empty conference room to the break room, hoping to find others hanging around. But at this hour, the whole building was mostly abandoned. A few agents had filtered in and out of the room, refilling coffee or grabbing something from the vending machine. They'd nodded at her and then continued on their errand, leaving her once again in the quiet.

She'd never had trouble being alone before. Actually preferred it most of the time. But right now, she'd give most anything for small talk with a perfect stranger. Something to keep her mind off Cash and his team walking into who knew what.

Would they find her sister? Or another clue? And what about Wade? Where could he be? Maya had checked in with Helene over an hour ago. Still no word on her husband's whereabouts. The worry and exhaustion were clear in the woman's voice.

Maya knew a thing or two about those feelings. Despite her amped-up nerves, fatigue pressed on her like an invisible weight. All of her usual coping mechanisms had failed. Pacing the room didn't help. She'd already tried it. Crossing her arms on the table, she rested her head on them and closed her eyes. Time to try something else. Something she hadn't done in a long time.

It had been years since she'd prayed. Did she believe God would hear her? That He would help?

Maybe not. But maybe He would.

God, please help me. I need to find my sister. And Wade. You know where they both are. Please give me a clue. Something that will lead me to them.

Her words felt rusty. Stale. Even a bit fake. But her heart meant it. And hopefully that would make a difference.

Pushing away from the table, she crossed the room to rinse her cup in the sink.

Her phone buzzed, and she grabbed it.

Not Cash.

She didn't recognize the number, but it could be someone else from his team.

"Hello?"

"Miss Reid?" a female voice said.

"Yes."

"It's Skylar… Laurel's roommate."

"Of course, I remember you." Why would Skylar be calling her at almost midnight? Unless— "Have you heard from Laurel?"

"Well, no. Not exactly. I'm at Aces. The club in Dansby."

"Okay…?"

"I thought I saw Laurel."

"What?" Maya's chest tightened and her voice jumped an octave.

"It was only for a second, but it looked so much like her."

Doubt warred with hope. Could it be possible that Laurel would show up in Dansby so many weeks after disappearing?

Maya wanted so much to believe it could.

"Stay there," she said. "I'm on my way." She grabbed her keys, thankful she'd insisted on driving her rental car to the station this morning.

Turning the ignition, she hesitated. Should she call Cash? He would try to talk her out of it. Or insist on going with her.

No time to wait on him. Laurel could be gone by then. And Maya wouldn't take that risk.

She shot off a quick text: Possible Laurel sighting at Aces. Call me when you get this.

He would be mad, but she didn't care. Not after the way he'd left her behind.

She'd faced dangerous situations many times. Solo. She was trained. Capable. Laurel needed her, and she was going to save her sister once and for all.

It was time she reminded herself that she didn't need anyone. Especially not Cash Brenner.

Cash leaned against Owen's car, letting the cool night air wash over him. Sweat clung to him. His face, his chest, his uniform.

The gold necklace. That had been the key.

And the one thing his brain had kept from him.

His mind had rejected the memory. Why? To protect him? The truth hurt. Gut-wrenching pain washed over him again.

Elizabeth was gone. Most likely dead all these years. He'd been chasing a ghost.

A heavy hand rested on his shoulder. He didn't have to look up to know it was Overstreet. His commander remained silent. No words were needed.

Cash had failed.

The realization swept over him, threatening to take him down once again.

What he wouldn't give for a little amnesia right now.

"We can finish up here," Overstreet said. "You and Owen head back to the office."

"Sir, I'm fine. I can stay."

Something akin to a growl came from his boss.

Cash looked up.

Overstreet's expression was stern, but his eyes softened. "You're not." He held up a hand to stem Cash's coming protest. "But you will be. In time. Right now, you need to go back. Talk to Maya. She'll be crawling the walls by now." One corner of his mouth ticked upward.

He was right. Maya was waiting for him. Wondering if he'd found Laurel.

For once, he was glad the answer to that was no.

But he would still have to tell her about the holding pens. About Elizabeth.

And once the bones had been processed and a positive ID made, he'd have to break the news to Elizabeth's family.

Fresh pain consumed him, clenching his gut.

Owen and Addie approached. Owen raised a brow, his questions unspoken. Cash nodded his answer. He was all right.

Addie came right at him, pulling him into a hug before he could protest.

He gave her a smile, then got into the car. Owen cranked the engine, and they headed for the station.

Time to face the music.

"I'll call Maya and let her know we're on the way back." He dug his phone out of the side pocket of his tactical pants and saw the missed message. "I have a text from her." He opened the app and read her words, his blood turning to ice. "She didn't..."

"What?"

He read the message aloud.

Owen shook his head. "Not good, man."

Cash ground his teeth as he dialed her number. It rang four times, and then her voice mail picked up.

"Maya, it's me. Call me back. I'm heading to Aces. Seriously, call me now."

He hung up and dialed two more times but only got voice mail. He then texted, but no answer came.

Worry churned in his gut.

She didn't say how she'd got the information about Laurel being spotted at the club. Someone must have called. But who?

The whole thing felt wrong. Laurel showing up at Aces out of the blue, after they'd been searching for her all these weeks... It sounded too good to be true. Which meant it probably was.

He sent up a string of prayers as Owen sped through the night.

Maya could be walking right into a trap.

The bass music thumped into her chest as Maya made her way through the crowd. Past midnight, but the club was busy with college students and others out for a good time. She'd had to wait in line for fifteen minutes to get in.

Her texts to Skylar had gone unanswered. Had she left already? Maya had asked her to stay and wait for her.

The young woman had sounded worried on the phone. Possibly seeing her missing roommate had to be upsetting, especially if it did turn out to be Laurel.

The thought sent Maya's heart into a gallop.

She scanned the crowd, searching for Skylar or Laurel, but the place was too packed. People pressed her from every side. She pushed her way through to the bar and checked those waiting to be served. Recognizing no one, she made her way to the edge and flagged down a server.

"I'm looking for Skylar Hudson." She had to yell to be heard over the crowd and the music. "Do you know her?"

The young man shook his head, then went back to working.

Maya pulled out her phone. Three missed calls from Cash, a voice mail, and two texts.

Owen and I are on our way to Aces. Call me.

Maya—call me. Now.

He wasn't happy that she'd left without him.

Of course not, but two could play that game.

She hesitated with her finger over the voice mail button. If he had information about Laurel, he wouldn't put it in the text, right?

Maybe. Or maybe not. She hit the button to listen to his voice mail. It was almost impossible to hear over the noise in the club, but she gathered that he was on his way. He didn't mention having new information to share.

She should call him back. But she would have to leave the building to even be able to hear him. And she wasn't leaving just yet—not until she found Skylar...or Laurel.

Another server brushed past, and Maya grabbed the young woman by the arm. "Hey, do you know Skylar Hudson?"

The woman shook her head, but Maya held up a finger, clicking over to a social media app and pulling up Skylar's profile. She held the phone for the woman to see.

She nodded. "Oh, yeah, I've seen her around before."

"Have you seen her tonight?"

The woman paused, then nodded. "I think so."

At least Skylar was around here somewhere. Maya clicked again. "How about this one? Laurel DeWitt. Have you seen her tonight?"

The woman checked the profile photo but shook her head. "I don't think so. Not tonight."

Maya's hope faded.

"But," the woman said, "it's really busy. Maybe I missed her."

Maybe. Or maybe Skylar was mistaken. Or sending Maya on a wild-goose chase.

But why? What would be the point of that?

She needed to find Skylar. And pushing through the crowd wasn't going to cut it.

Grabbing a chair, she climbed onto it and then on top of a table, looking out over the mass of people.

Starting with those on the dance floor, she scanned faces. Then she checked the perimeter of the room.

There! Finally. Near the hallway that led to the restrooms. Skylar stood with her back against the wall, arms crossed.

Why hadn't she answered Maya's texts?

She made her way through the crowd to Skylar.

The young woman's eyes widened as she approached. "You're here!"

"I said I was coming. I texted you."

"You did?" She checked her phone. "I guess I missed it. I don't get good reception in here."

Maya had an odd feeling Skylar wasn't being truthful. But if the young woman had called her here, why would she lie about it now?

Either way, she was ready for some answers.

She moved closer, and the thumping of the music dissipated a little this far back from the dance floor. "Where did you see Laurel?"

"I'm not positive it was her." She shrugged, shifting her gaze. "I mean, it could've been someone who looked like her."

Skylar had sounded almost frantic on the phone. She'd been sure enough that she'd called Maya to come down here. Why was she changing her story now?

Was she playing some kind of sick game?

No matter. Maya would go along with it if it meant finding her sister.

"Of course. But it wouldn't hurt to check it out, right? So, where did you see who you thought might be Laurel?"

Skylar paused, then sighed, seeming to come to a decision. "I saw her across the room about an hour after I got here."

"Did you talk to her?"

"No. Like I said, it looked like her. I started over, but she turned and headed back there." She thumbed toward the hallway. "I checked the bathroom, but I didn't see her. That's when I called you. And planted myself out here in case she came out again."

"But she hasn't?"

"No."

It had taken Maya a half hour to drive from Gadden Valley to Dansby. Maybe the Laurel lookalike worked here, and she was taking her break.

Or maybe it was Laurel, and she was on something. Passed out in a back room.

The urge to find her sister flowed hot. If Laurel was in this club, Maya wasn't leaving here without her.

"Okay, let's go."

"Where?"

"We're going to check every room in this hallway."

"We?" Skylar's eyes widened. "Why do I have to go?"

Maya raised an eyebrow. "Don't you want to find your friend?"

"Oh, of course." She shrugged. "I meant…don't you want me to wait here in case she comes out? What if you miss her?"

Maya had seen backpedaling before. She wasn't sure what kind of game Skylar was playing, but she'd feel better if she kept an eye on the young woman.

"The hallway is small. I don't think we'd miss her. Come on." Grabbing Skylar's arm, Maya pushed her ahead. "Show me which way she went."

"Well, like I said, she went down the hall. By the time I got across the room, I couldn't tell where she'd gone. I assumed she went to the restroom, so I checked there. But I didn't look in any other room. I mean, I don't have that kind of authority."

Technically, neither did Maya. But she wasn't going to let a door keep her from her sister.

Starting on the right, Maya checked each door. One was a storage closet. The next was locked. The sign read Manager's Office. If she didn't find Laurel, she'd circle back to the manager and demand he open it.

The room at the other end of the hall was the security office, where they'd checked out the camera footage the night they'd seen Dillon with the other missing woman. She could ask the manager to let her view tonight's recordings and see if she could spot the woman Skylar thought was Laurel.

"Okay, let's go find the manager."

"Wait," Skylar said. "What about that door?"

Maya eyed it. "Looks like an emergency exit."

"Do you think she could have gone outside? Maybe she left."

Maya had considered that possibility. But wouldn't the alarm have sounded? Stepping closer, she didn't see a sign that warned it would. "It couldn't hurt to check."

Pushing open the door, she waited for a blaring siren. Nothing happened. The door opened to a back parking lot. A couple of dumpsters and a few cars. But no people.

"Anything?" Skylar asked from the doorway.

"Nothing."

Disappointment reared, but she wasn't giving up so easily.

"I think I'll take a closer look around," she said. "Make sure we don't miss anything."

Skylar nodded. "I can go find the manager."

"Thanks." Maya surveyed the lot. An alleyway led behind the building. Clicking on her phone's flashlight, she began making a slow sweep of the area.

A rustling sound had her whipping around. A small, orange cat scooted around the dumpster and sped off into the alley.

Maya blew out a breath to steady her nerves. She was jumpy, but after the past week, she had reason to be. Her determination to find Laurel overrode everything at this point. Still… She knelt to retrieve the gun in her ankle holster.

Suddenly, a hand reached around her, holding a cloth over her nose and mouth. A sickly, sweet smell overwhelmed her as something sharp and painful hit her in the neck.

The world began to blur.

ELEVEN

Cash steered Owen's sedan into the parking lot of Skylar Hudson's apartment complex. When he couldn't find Maya at the club or reach her by phone, he'd called Overstreet. The rest of their team had arrived, and he and Owen had left them working the scene.

He refused to call it a crime scene.

It couldn't be. He had to hold out hope that Maya was following a lead on her own.

Which was what he had to do. Follow every lead to find her.

Right now, the only lead he had was Skylar Hudson. She was the last person who'd been with Maya at Aces, according to the security footage.

The memory of being here a few days ago with Maya floated through his mind. Working with her the past couple of weeks had been…well, he couldn't say it had been fun. Or even enjoyable. Because they were now looking for two missing women—Laurel and Kellie.

Yet, he couldn't deny how much he appreciated spending time with her. Maya was unlike any other woman he'd dated. Strong, smart, independent. But there was something else about her underneath the bravado. A tender heart. Loving, caring. Even though he knew her life hadn't been easy.

She had scars no one could see. Like him. Wounds beneath

the surface. Wrapped around his heart. A barrier to the outside world.

He'd seen glimpses of that in Maya. Her pain mirrored his own. She understood him like no one else ever had.

And he'd never forgive himself if something happened to her.

Finding her was priority one.

He banged on the apartment door. "Skylar Hudson."

It was two o'clock in the morning, but he didn't care who he woke. He pounded again. "GBI. Open the door."

A light clicked on inside.

"It's Special Agent Cash Brenner," he said when she peeked through the blinds.

The door lock clicked. Still dressed. Skylar hadn't been sleeping. But she had been crying, based on her puffy eyes and red nose.

"Can I help you?" she asked, her voice hoarse.

"Sorry to bother you so late. Special Agent Brenner. I was here the other day."

"I remember."

Cash motioned toward Owen. "This is my partner, Agent Donnelly. We need to ask you some questions."

"I already told you what I know."

"It's not about Laurel," he said. "Maya… Miss Reid…is missing." His gut clenched at the words.

Skylar crossed her arms but averted her gaze. "Why would I know anything about that?"

He was in no mood for beating around the bush. All cards on the table. "Because you were at Aces with her tonight. We saw you on the security camera. Where is Maya?"

Her eyes widened. "All right, yes. I was at Aces tonight. I thought I saw Laurel, so I called Miss Reid." She held her hands out at her sides. "But we looked around and… I guess I was just mistaken."

"So, you both left?"

"Yes."

"You saw her leave?"

Owen pulled out his phone. "I can pull up the security footage to jog your memory."

"I didn't actually see her leave. I went to get the manager. When we got back, I couldn't find her, I figured she gave up and went home." Skylar crossed her arms.

Defensive move.

Her story tracked. They had seen Skylar go out the back door a couple of minutes after Maya. But Skylar had reentered and left. Maya had not.

"Have you heard from her since then?"

"No."

Cash ground his teeth. They were losing time.

Owen stepped forward. "You seem upset. Everything okay?"

"I…broke up with…someone." She sniffed.

This was getting them nowhere. "I need to find Maya. Please, help me."

Swiping at her cheeks, she lifted her head. "You love her, don't you?"

"I—" He swallowed. His mind and heart had been edging around the word for days, but he'd refused to give it a voice. But hearing Skylar say it had solidified it. "I do."

Pain pierced his heart. He had to tell her. Come clean about his true feelings. Even if it terrified him.

"Please." He gripped her hands between his. "I think she's in trouble."

A fresh flow of tears fell. "I didn't know what he was— He just said to call her. That was all. I didn't know he would… He promised—" Her words jumbled as she cried in earnest.

It had been a setup. He was right. Someone had used Skylar to lure Maya to the club. A new wave of fear washed over him. Maya had been taken.

* * *

Maya's body hurt all over. That was her first thought. She was tired. So exhausted. Her legs felt weak, like she'd run a marathon. Her arms were too heavy to lift. So were her eyelids.

"Miss Reid?"

A voice floated through the fog around her mind. She knew that voice. Who was it? She tried to remember.

Masculine. Strong. Authoritative.

"Miss Reid? Open your eyes."

She willed her body to obey. Forced her eyelids to open.

A room. Small with metal walls. Gray. Drab. Like she was in some kind of metal building.

A single fluorescent bulb hung overhead. Too bright. She closed her eyes against the offending light.

"No. Don't close your eyes again. Look at me."

That voice again.

Maya wanted to sleep. To escape into the darkness. But the voice pulled at her. And so did the sense that something was very wrong.

She opened her eyes and glanced down. Her wrists were tied to the armrests of an office chair that had seen better days, the fake leather cracked and peeling. Her legs were bound at the ankles. Instinct had her struggling against the ties.

"Don't bother. There's no getting loose."

Turning her head toward the voice, she saw him.

Dark brown eyes. Steely gray hair.

Wade DeWitt sat in a chair across from her.

What was he doing here? And where *was* here?

Her muddled thoughts began to jell. Wade was on the run. They'd been searching for him. Then the phone call. From Skylar. Maya had gone to that club to find Laurel. Walked out the exit door. The alley.

Then...blackness.

She had been knocked out. Probably with some kind of drug, given the woozy way she felt right now.

And then brought here. By Wade?

He was looking at her now, but his eyes weren't cold or hard.

They were…worried.

"Miss Reid?" he asked again. This time, she heard the concern in his voice.

"Wade?" Her voice cracked. She swallowed against her dry throat. "Mr. DeWitt?"

"Wade is fine," he said. "I think we're far past any civilities now."

Sitting across from her in another version of her own chair, he watched her. But something was off.

He looked awful. Hair disheveled. Unshaven. The light blue dress shirt he'd been wearing in his office days ago now wrinkled and stained. And his arms were angled behind him in an unnatural way.

Then she realized. His feet were bound at the ankles. His arms must be tied behind him as well.

He wasn't holding her in this odd place. Wade DeWitt was a prisoner, same as herself.

And they had been terribly wrong about him.

"Where are we?" she asked.

"I'm not exactly sure. My guess is one of my warehouses. This looks like the inside of the shipping containers we use for the import-export business."

"How long have you been here?"

"Hard to say. With no windows, I can't tell day from night."

Of course. That made sense. Maya looked around. She had no idea how long she'd been knocked out.

"When did I get here?"

"I estimate it's been an hour or so. When they brought you in, you were unconscious. Then they shot something into your arm, and you started waking up a little after that."

The pain in the alley. Something sharp had stung her neck before the world had gone dark. They'd given her an injection of some kind.

"Who brought me in here?"

"Again, I can't say. They were wearing ski masks. Two men, I'd guess, by their height and build."

"Is that how you got here, too?"

"Probably. The last thing I remember was the day you and that other detective came to my office. I had a meeting downtown, so after you left, I got into the elevator, but then everything went dark. When I woke up, I was here."

They'd thought Wade had disappeared because he was guilty.

But he wasn't the perpetrator. He'd been kidnapped and brought here. He was a victim.

Like she was.

Taken. Held hostage.

With no one to know where she was.

She never should have gone to the club alone. Should've waited for Cash, like he'd asked.

Cash. Where was he now? Out looking for her, probably. Would he even know where to start?

It had hurt, being left behind. Left out of the raid of the old warehouse. Even when they'd searched Wade's building, she had sulked while waiting in the security office.

But Cash wasn't trying to exclude her. Not pushing her away. It was clear to see now. He'd been trying to protect her. Keep her out of danger.

And for good reasons, based on her current situation.

But where had his efforts gotten him? He was probably frantic with worry now. Searching for her like they'd been searching for Wade.

Would they be able to find her? They hadn't been able to find Wade so far. No one would know to look for them here. Wherever this was.

If only she'd listened to Cash. Trusted him.

But she'd been afraid to trust him. He had hurt her before. And she had let their past influence her behavior in the present. She had built up a wall to keep him out. It was easier that way.

Her feelings for him terrified her. But the thought of never seeing him again terrified her more.

"We've got to get out of here." She pulled against the ties around her wrists.

"It's no use. I've tried."

"There has to be a way. Somehow." She wasn't going to die in here. Laurel could still be alive, and Maya needed to find her.

And face her feelings for Cash.

She scanned for something she could use to break free. The storage container was set up like a room. Could almost pass for an office, even if a stark and dreary one. Besides the two chairs she and Wade were strapped in, there was an old metal desk. Maybe there was something in one of the drawers she could use. Using her legs as leverage, she scooted her chair inch by inch toward the desk.

"What are you doing?" Wade asked.

"I'm going to see if I can get these drawers open. Maybe find something to cut through the restraints."

"Great idea," Wade said, shaking his head. "I hadn't even thought of that."

He'd probably never had to break out of anywhere, unlike Maya, who had found herself in tight spots before. Back in the day, she'd been known as quite the escape artist, which hadn't exactly endeared her to her many foster parents.

With her hands tied to the arms of the chair, her range of motion was nil. Instead, she pulled her tied legs up to her chest and hooked the toe of her boot under the drawer handle.

"You're quite resourceful," Wade said.

She'd had to be, growing up in foster homes. Fighting for everything she had. Struggling to survive. But there was no use going into that with Wade now. Instead, she pulled at the middle drawer. Locked.

Shifting to the side, she tried to next drawer. "It might be a wasted effort, but it couldn't hurt to try."

The small drawer wasn't locked. Maya gave it a hard tug. The drawer pulled out of the desk and dropped to the floor with a loud clang.

Papers scattered on the floor, but she spied something long, thin and metal just under corner of the desk.

"I think that's a letter opener," she said. "If I can get my shoe off, I might be able to grab it with my toes."

A loud scraping noise echoed around the metal walls as the door of the container opened.

Maya froze and steeled herself to face whoever came through the door.

A man wearing a black ski mask entered. He strode up to Maya and looked her over with dark eyes. "You're awake." He glanced at the drawer on the floor. "And busy, I see." He made a tsking sound.

Something about his voice, his demeanor, felt familiar, but her muddled mind couldn't recall where she'd seen or heard him before.

"Where's my sister?"

The man tipped his head, watching her. "Not the question I expected. Usually, it's who am I? What do I want? Where are we? And then the begging starts." He mimicked a high-pitched voice. "Please let me go. Please don't hurt me."

Her stomach turned at the callousness. But she wouldn't give him the satisfaction. "I'm not afraid of you." She maintained eye contact, not willing to back down.

One corner of his mouth tipped upward. "You really are something, aren't you?" He reached a gloved hand toward her, but she jerked her head away. Her defiance only seemed to amuse him. He chuckled darkly. "Oh, we're going to have some fun with you."

Maya focused on the only thing that mattered. "Where is my sister?" she asked again. She had to know if Laurel was still alive. If she was, maybe Maya could strike a bargain with her captors.

Herself in exchange for her sister's freedom.

If Laurel was dead…well, then it didn't matter what they did to Maya now. There would be no reason to fight her way out.

Cash's face floated to her mind, but she pushed it aside.

The man leaned over her, resting his hands on the arms of the chair. "Now, if I told you, where would be the fun in that?"

His cologne wafted over her, the scent filling her nostrils and triggering a memory.

Her stomach dropped as realization dawned.

Pulling back, she lurched forward, using her forehead to smash into his nose.

He roared as he fell backward. Grabbing the mask, he ripped it from his head. Blood poured from his broken nose. With red dripping down his chin and dark bruises forming under his eyes, he looked much worse for the wear.

But Maya would recognize him anywhere.

Dillon Cordell glared at her with eyes full of hate.

Desperation clawed at him, but Cash stuffed the emotion down.

Skylar Hudson had been in the interrogation room for an hour.

After admitting to luring Maya to the club, she'd asked for a lawyer and gone silent.

His phone rang. The number wasn't one he recognized.

He slipped from the room.

"Brenner." He answered and held his breath, hoping for the voice on the other line to be Maya's.

"Agent Brenner? This is Helene DeWitt."

His pulse spiked. "Have you heard from your husband?"

"No. Well, not exactly. I..." Her voice was weak and trembly. "I don't know if this will be helpful, but I thought you should know...in case."

"Any information is valuable right now."

She let out a breath. "I saw a notification a moment ago, in Wade's email inbox. I was able to get into his account and check his messages."

No activity had been noted on Wade's phone since he'd disappeared from his building. They assumed the phone had been turned off. Same as Maya's.

Not for the first time, he wondered if Wade had taken her.

"That's great, Helene. What was it?"

"An alert from the security company we use to monitor our properties. It said an incorrect pass code had been entered on the security keypad."

"At Wade's office?"

"No. That was the strange part. It was for a building in Greenley. We used it as extra storage for the import-export business, but we sold it last year. I guess the security company never updated the contact email."

Cash's mind turned with possibilities.

"There was another notification a minute later," Helene continued. "That said the correct code had been entered. So, it could have been a random mistake."

Or it could be DeWitt using the facility. Wade wasn't stupid. He had to know they were looking for him. A building he had access to that wasn't listed in his name would be a good place to hide out.

"When did the notifications come in?"

"Around four this morning."

A few hours after Maya had disappeared from Ace's. If Wade

had taken her, or had someone else do it for him, it was reasonable they could have brought Maya to Greenley.

It was a long shot, but he would take any opportunity to find her.

"Helene, do you remember the name of the company you sold the building to?"

"I do. It was an odd name. Nyne Lyves, spelled with *y*'s."

The name of the corporation Maya had uncovered. Agent Chandler had discovered it was a shell company and was still trying to track down the owner. Cash's pulse spiked. Maya needed him to find her.

And he needed her. More than he ever imagined possible. "Could you give me the address for the warehouse?"

He thanked her, disconnected and hurried back to the interrogation room. Skylar was gone.

"Where is she?" he asked Owen.

"In holding. The lawyer convinced her to take a deal. We got a name." He leveled a look at Cash. "Dillon Cordell."

"But…he's…"

"Apparently not as dead as we thought."

He would be, if Cash ever got his hands on him. "How?"

"He showed up at her apartment and claimed he had to fake his death to get the police off his back. Said he'd been set up and that Maya was the only one who could prove his innocence. He convinced Skylar to lure Maya to the club to help him."

"Why would she do that?" That seemed a far stretch.

"Skylar was interested in Dillon first, but he chose Laurel instead."

Cash recalled Skylar's behavior when he and Maya had questioned her about Laurel's disappearance. She'd seemed more angry than worried. "I can see Skylar wanting to get back at Laurel, but that still seems a lot to ask."

"Dillon promised her they could be together once everything was cleared up. He said he only dated Laurel because he'd been paid to."

"Paid?" Cash's brows rose. "By Wade?"

Owen shrugged. "She didn't know, and it may have been another lie. But when she took Maya to Dillon, he knocked her out with some kind of drug, shoved her into a van and took off."

Cash's panic returned at the thought of Maya drugged once again. He prayed it wasn't an overdose like last time. The need to find her was almost overwhelming.

"But she has no idea where he took Maya."

"I might." He explained the phone call from Helene DeWitt. "I'm going to check it out."

"I'll call Overstreet on the way." Owen clapped a hand on Cash's shoulder. "We'll find her."

He prayed his friend was right.

TWELVE

"Dillon?" Wade stared at their captor with wide eyes. "But… they said you were dead."

"That's what he wanted us to believe." Maya kept her eyes on the much-alive Dillon Cordell. He'd somehow managed to blow up his own car, almost taking her and Cash with it. But he'd escaped, leaving them to believe he'd been killed. And with the car still being processed by the GBI, probably no one had realized there wasn't a body.

Now he glared at her, his dark eyes full of hate. He wiped blood from his nose. "You're going to pay for that."

He lunged at her. Maya brought her knees to her chest and shoved her feet into his abdomen, sending him into the metal wall.

With another growl, he rallied, heading for her again.

"Stop!" The command came from the doorway. "I told you Miss Reid was off-limits."

Dillon froze, and Maya turned toward the voice.

A gasp escaped from Wade, and his voice came out in a whisper. "Audra?"

His secretary stood before them, her form bearing authority.

"I don't understand." Wade's expression held as much shock as Maya felt. "Why?"

Audra Peterson entered the small compartment and joined

Dillon, who was holding his abdomen from where Maya had kicked him.

His injuries brought a little satisfaction. No telling the kinds of pain he had inflicted on his victims.

"Why? I'll tell you why, Wade." Audra spit the words at her boss, her voice full of contained fury. "Because for decades, I've worked for you. Taken care of your business. Done your bidding. Served you." The last words came out as part sneer and part snarl. She stood over Wade, her slight form trembling with anger. "And for what? What did I get in return?"

"I—I…paid you a good salary." The man looked up at his captor in confusion. "I was a good boss…wasn't I?"

"You were." Audra took a step back. "But that was the problem, Wade. *You* were the boss. I wasn't." She crossed her arms. "And I was never going to be. Never going to be anything but your little secretary."

"And you wanted more." The words shot out before Maya could check them.

"Exactly." Pride shone in Audra's eyes. "I found a way to make my own fortune. And I used Wade's business to do it. Right under his nose."

"How?" Wade asked.

"Working in your export business, I made a few, shall we say, unsavory acquaintances. And I found out where the real money was."

"Human trafficking?" Wade's voice broke with disbelief.

"It made the most sense. I have access to your transport trucks. I had them altered with hidden compartments."

"Dillon." Maya's gaze cut to him. He had the skills from his job at the auto body shop. "And you used him to lure the victims."

"Turns out, he was good for more than just the repair work." Audra slid her eyes to Maya, taking a few steps in her direction. "It may be the twenty-first century, but it's still a man's world. The only way for a woman to get ahead is to make her own way. To take control. You know what I'm talking about."

Disgust and anger churned in Maya's gut. "And your idea of girl power is to, what? Sell other women to the highest bidder?"

Eyes narrowing, Audra shook her head. "Not all women are created equal. The ones I take could never understand power. Never stand on their own two feet. My mother was like that. Drifting from man to man. Searching for someone to complete her. These women think they need a man to validate their existence. I'm only giving them what they want."

"Including my sister? You'd put Laurel in that class?" Anger shivered through her veins.

"Oh." Audra waved a dismissive hand. "Laurel was simply… a problem that needed to be dealt with."

Wade stiffened in his chair. "How's that?"

"She came by the office one day when you were out, overheard a conversation she shouldn't have. I played it off, convincing her that she had misunderstood. But I could see it in her eyes. Suspicion. I knew she wouldn't forget so easily. So… I sent Dillon to distract her."

"You were only pretending to be interested in my daughter?"

Dillon laughed. "As if I'd ever be interested in a Goody Two-shoes like that."

Audra sighed. "You'd better go see about that nose. Looks like it might be broken. I can't have my star player disfigured. It's bad for business."

Tossing a glare Maya's way, Dillon left.

"So, you set Laurel up," Maya said. "To keep her off your trail. And the addiction? That was your doing, too, wasn't it?"

"Yes. When Dillon's charms seemed to be failing, I had to try something else. So, I arranged for a little accident."

"The ski trip," Wade said. "You tampered with Laurel's equipment?" His face flushed red with apparent anger.

"I couldn't just kill her. That would invite too much attention. An investigation. So, I tried to make it look like an accident, although it didn't go the way I intended. But it worked out all right. The doctor prescribed an opioid for her pain, and it was easy for Dillon to keep slipping those to her until she was addicted."

"You knew about her birth mother's addiction."

"Yes, and having your daughter take the same path kept you and Helene so worried and busy trying to help her, you stayed out of my business."

White-hot rage rolled over Maya. Her poor sister. Put through such torture so this horrible woman could cover up her deplorable crimes. Wade seemed to have a similar reaction as his eyes burned a hole in Audra.

"It was when she reached out to you—" Audra turned her gaze to Maya "—that I knew I had to get rid of her once and for all."

"Me?"

"The last thing I needed was a private investigator snooping around."

The familiar grip of guilt wrapped around Maya's heart. Once again, she had caused her sister trouble.

"But we hired someone to find her," Wade said.

He had? This was news to Maya. Wade had never mentioned hiring his own investigator, only that he wanted to keep Laurel's name out of the news.

Audra laughed. "You think that PI was real? He worked for me. And I made sure he fed you false information."

"And then, what?" Maya said. "You tried to kill me off, too?"

The truck that ran her off the bridge. The drugs laced into her tea. All of it had been orchestrated by Audra.

"I had to. We didn't know how much you and your GBI boyfriend knew."

"But none of it worked," Maya said. "So, you had Skylar lure me to the club. Was she in on it the whole time?"

"No. That was Dillon's idea. He fed her some lies and used her own jealousy against her. Seems she had a thing for him. It really dug at her when he started dating Laurel."

The anger Maya had seen in Skylar's eyes. She was mad at Laurel for stealing Dillon away.

"What did you give me, by the way?" Maya asked. "At the club? What did you drug me with?" It had felt different than the drugs Audra had laced into her tea.

"Oh, that? It's quite simple actually. Which is what makes it so brilliant. It's how I get all the girls." She reached into her pocket and pulled out a syringe. "It's insulin."

That was what the attacker had tried to put into Cash's IV at the hospital. It must have been Audra dressed as a nurse. "But I'm not diabetic."

"Exactly. When you give insulin to someone who isn't diabetic, it causes their blood sugar to drop drastically, and then they pass out. It's a simple way to render someone unconscious."

"And then you gave her something else to wake her up?" Wade asked.

"Glucose. It reverses the effects. Like I said. Simple but brilliant." She turned to Wade. "And I owe it all to you."

"Me?"

"Remember your dog Horatio?"

Understanding dawned on Wade's face. "He had diabetes."

"On one of our trips out to the kennel, I had an interesting chat with the veterinarian. He explained to me how insulin and glucose work in the system. He also warned of what could happen if insulin was given to the wrong dog. An idea formed, and the rest is history. Although it did take a bit of experimentation to find exactly the right doses." A frown pulled down her eyebrows. "But I've got it down to a science now."

"Good for us." Maya couldn't keep the sarcasm out of her voice.

Audra turned to her, eyes cold. "Yes, good for you, Miss Reid, as I chose not to kill you."

Maya sat up in the chair, matching the woman's steel. "And why is that?"

"Maybe I decided you're worth more alive than dead." Her eyes raked Maya up and down. "Someone like you will fetch a hefty price tag."

Maya wanted to throw up.

Audra turned to Wade. "And maybe I haven't figured out exactly how to kill you yet."

Wade's face blanched white. "Audra, please. I—"

"Boss?" A pale, thin man stuck his head around the corner of the compartment opening. "The buyers are here."

The word *buyers* had Maya swallowing back a gag.

"They're early." Audra shot the words like an accusation at the small man, then sighed. "Get the others ready. I'll be right there."

Others? Could Laurel be nearby? A sliver of hope spread through Maya's heart.

Audra turned, smoothing her sweater and running a hand over her hair. "I've got some business to attend to, and then I'll be back to…finish this." She gestured toward them.

Maya didn't plan on being here when the woman returned. She had to find Laurel.

As if reading her thoughts, Audra paused at the door. "And in case you get any bright ideas…" She snapped her fingers, and a large black dog appeared at her side.

A Doberman.

Like the one Cash had said chased him in the warehouse. It had been Audra who'd sent the dog after him that night.

"I'll leave my friend here to keep you company." Audra

snapped again and said some words Maya didn't understand before exiting.

The dog stood at attention inside the door, dark eyes sharp.

"What did she say? 'Pass out'?" Maya asked.

"Pass auf," Wade corrected. "It's a German command that means to watch or guard. It's very common in obedience training. I use it with my dogs."

"Must be where Audra picked it up. Know any German words for *we've got to get out of here*? Because I don't intend to stick around to find out what her plans for us are."

Maya pulled against her restraints once more, but it was a futile effort. If she could figure out a way to get that letter opener under the desk…

She scooted her chair closer. A deep growl came from the dog.

"I wouldn't do that if I were you," Wade said. "This dog appears highly trained. If she's anything like mine, she'll do whatever it takes to obey her master."

"We've got to do something, because I have a feeling those 'buyers' aren't here for office supplies."

Wade's face blanched another shade of pale. "You mean—"

"If we ever want to see Laurel again, we've got to find her before Audra completes her transaction." She scooted another inch closer to the desk and was met with another growl as the dog took a step towards her.

What was the likelihood she could reach the letter opener before the dog bit her hand off? Probably not good.

"Wade? You know any commands to tell the dog to stand down?"

"Actually, yes, I—" He tilted his head and gave the dog a long look.

"What?"

"It's just that— No, it couldn't be."

"Running out of time here."

He shook his head. "Sorry. For a moment, I thought maybe it was my dog. But that couldn't be. She died a few years ago. Nina was—"

The dog's ears stood up, and she turned her face toward Wade.

"Say the name again," Maya said.

"Nina?"

An almost imperceptible wag of the dog's cropped tail.

"It is you!" Wade's voice held amazement. "Nina!"

"Shh!" Maya said. "Keep your voice down."

The door to the compartment was still open, and she wasn't sure how close Audra might be.

"Nina, *aus*," Wade said in a lower volume.

The dog's stance relaxed.

"I think that worked. What did you say to her?"

"*Aus* means to stop what she's doing. Basically, undoing the command Audra gave her to guard us."

"Not much of a guard dog if anyone who knows the command could tell her to stop."

"Actually, it's not that simple. Nina would only comply for someone she views as her master. Which for now is Audra. But what she probably didn't plan on was me recognizing my dog, or her recognizing me. Nina still remembers me as her master."

"Wunderbar," Maya said. "She know any other tricks? Like maybe pick up that letter opener and bring it to me?"

"Shouldn't be a problem. But she'll need to know what we want her to get. See if you can slide it to me with your foot."

Maya maneuvered to the desk, then pressed her foot over the silver file and slid it toward Wade.

He touched it with the tip of his foot. "Nina, *fetch*."

The dog obeyed, grasping the tool in her mouth and dropping it onto Wade's lap.

"*Braver hund!* Good dog!" Wade praised the dog now sitting at his feet.

"Fetch? Really?" Maya said. "I could've told her that."

"She wouldn't have obeyed you."

"Right." Maya scooted as close as she could to Wade's chair and grasped the letter opener in her right hand, still tied to the arm of the chair. "Okay, let's see if this will work. Can you turn around so I can reach your binds?"

Wade complied, and Maya worked the letter opener on the plastic ties around his wrist. It was awkward and slow, and she poked him more than once. But other than a sharp inhale a time or two, Wade kept silent.

"Sorry," Maya said.

"It's fine. Whatever it takes to get free and find my daughter."

How had she ever thought this man callous as to his daughter's well-being? It was clear now how much he loved her. She had misunderstood his reluctance for publicity as concern for his own reputation when he had actually been working behind the scenes to find Laurel.

Finally, the ties snapped, and Wade turned in his chair, arms free.

"Undo the ties on your ankles, then get mine."

Maya's pulse raced as Wade worked to cut her binds. She itched to get free and find her sister. Every second was precious.

The final tie snapped, and she sprinted to the door. Wade and the dog were right behind her. "Stay here. Let me scout it out."

She slipped out the door and into a large room. It appeared to be some kind of warehouse, stacked with shipping containers like the one they were in. She turned in a circle. How would they find Laurel?

Something cold and hard wedged into her temple. A gun.

"Don't move." Dillon's words were filled with anger.

Cash held his weapon at the ready as he and his team approached the building on silent feet. They walked single file, with Cash leading the line. Behind him were Owen, Addie,

Agent Watts, and a few officers from the Greenley Police Department.

SAC Overstreet commanded the operation from a few yards away, coordinating with the Greenley police chief and their SWAT team.

ASAC Hasler radioed that his team had reached the other end of the building and were ready for Cash's call to breach. Agent Chandler had confirmed the alarm system was off.

Cash acknowledged their positions, waited a count of five, and then spoke quietly into his mic. "Breach."

Owen used a pry bar to force open the back door, and Cash was through the doorway in an instant. The quiet, dark warehouse met him. Not the same as the warehouse in the industrial park, but close enough to trigger a reaction. Flashbacks from the night he'd lost his memory flew at him, but he pushed ahead, focusing on one thing.

Find Maya.

He wasn't about to lose her now.

After he gave the hand signal for his team to spread out, they made their way through the building. Owen stayed with him as Addie and Watts went right and the officers from Greenley PD went left. Cash slipped through a doorway into another room with a few overhead lights on.

Large metal shipping containers were stacked toward the ceiling, and heavy-duty equipment sat idle. This had to be the way the trafficking ring was transporting their captives.

His stomach roiled at the idea of such suffering, but he couldn't get distracted from his mission. If all went well, they would rescue the kidnapped, take down the ring, and reunite Maya with her sister.

It was a big ask, but he kept up a steady thread of prayer that they could do all three.

Noise from the other end of the building reached his earpiece. Hasler's team had either been discovered or found their targets.

Stealth was no longer necessary. "Move out!" he commanded his team, and they rushed forward.

Movement came from his left. He ducked behind a pillar, went low and surveyed the figure emerging from one of the shipping containers a few yards away. A woman.

She glanced both ways from the entrance of the container.

Maya.

His heart swelled at the sight of her. Arms itched to hold her.

He stood to go to her as another figure emerged from the shadows behind her. And put a gun to her head.

"Maya!" he shouted her name as he trained his weapon on her captor.

The man swiveled, putting Maya between them, using her as a shield.

Dillon Cordell. A white splint covered his nose, purple bruises under his eyes. But he was alive, as Skylar had said. Fury surged through him.

"Put the gun down!" Owen shouted from a couple feet away.

On his other side, Addie held her weapon at the ready.

"I'll do it, man," Cordell said, digging the gun into Maya's temple. "One more step, and she's a goner."

Maya's eyes stared into his. Not the fear he expected. Instead, her eyes softened as she looked at him. Overwhelming love and fear rose in his chest.

He couldn't let her down. Not this time.

Releasing his hold on the trigger, he signaled to Dillon. "I'm putting my gun down. Let her go." Cash placed his weapon on the ground in front of him and held up his hands.

"All of you." Dillon waved his gun toward Cash's team.

No one moved. With Cash unarmed, they would hold their positions.

"I said put them down." Dillon's voice held a thread of desperation that Cash didn't like.

An unstable suspect was a dangerous one.

"I'm afraid they can't do that, Dillon. As long as you have a weapon, my team needs to protect me. But if you'll put your gun down, we can work this out."

"No way." Dillon tightened his hold on Maya. "They'll shoot me."

"No one wants that, I can assure you." A shoot-out would put Maya in the crossfire. He motioned to Owen. "Fall back."

His partner took a few steps backward but kept his aim steady.

Cash ran scenarios in his head, trying to come up with a way to disarm Dillon that didn't put Maya at risk. *God, help me save her.*

He would lay it all on the line, face his fears, if it meant having Maya in his life. Nothing compared with the thought of losing her.

She caught his gaze, her eyes seeming to try to convey a message. Flicking her eyes to the shadows, she gave the slightest nod. Then, turning back to him, she mouthed something.

Her silent words hit him harder than a bullet.

I love you.

A dark flash bolted from the container. A Doberman! Cash froze. It looked like the same one who'd attacked him in Pendleton. And now it lunged at Dillon, jaws clamping down on the arm that held the gun.

A deep scream came from Dillon as he went down, pulling Maya with him.

Cash dropped and grabbed his gun as a shot echoed in the room.

"Maya!" He raced to her, heart thumping.

The dog held fast to Dillon, who lay across an unmoving Maya.

No! God, please!

"Nina, *aus*!"

Stop. Cash recognized the German command used by K-9 handlers as he registered Wade DeWitt standing nearby.

The dog released Dillon and sat on its haunches.

Cash's mind registered the commotion as Owen secured DeWitt. Addie called for the paramedics who were on standby with Overstreet. But he had only one thought.

"Maya?" Pushing Dillon over, he knelt beside her. Blood covered her chest. His heart stopped. Hands shook as he pressed against her neck.

Her gentle pulse thrummed beneath his fingers. Long lashes fluttered as her eyes opened.

"Cash." His name on her lips sent warmth flooding through him.

She started to sit up.

"Easy, honey. You've been shot."

She touched her chest, confusion creasing her brow. "No, I haven't."

He turned to where Dillon lay on the ground, gunshot wound in the abdomen. Shot with his own weapon. Owen worked to staunch the blood while Addie directed the paramedics who had entered the room.

"Is he…?" he asked.

"Still alive," Addie said.

Cash expelled a breath, turning to Maya. She reached for him, and he gathered her in his arms. Held her to him and closed his eyes. *Thank You, God.*

She leaned back, pressing her hands to his face. "You found me."

His throat tightened. He swallowed. "Always."

And he was never going to lose her again.

Maya willed her racing heart to slow as she kept her arms laced around Cash's neck. His embrace sent warmth through her icy limbs. She breathed in, the scent of his aftershave mingling with the acrid smell of gunfire. And blood.

But not hers. *Thank You, God, for saving me. For sending Cash to find me.*

She'd really thought she would die. Could still feel the cold, hard metal of Dillon's gun pressed into her temple. The panic in Cash's eyes. And the flash of desperation in Wade's as he'd sent Nina to her rescue.

Dillon could have shot the dog. Or Maya. When they'd fallen to the floor, the gun had fired with a jolt. Her ears rang from the blast. She had expected a bullet to slash through her body. But the slug had lodged into Dillon instead.

Breaking from Cash's hold, she glanced toward the form on the ground. Surrounded by law enforcement and paramedics working to save his life.

Cash stroked her hair. "You good?"

She nodded, unsure if her voice would work.

The radio attached at his shoulder crackled. "We've got the buyers. East side of the building."

He keyed the mic to respond. "Copy that. Suspect is down. Repeat, Cordell in custody. One GSW to the abdomen."

"Can he talk?"

Maya recognized SAC Overstreet's voice.

"Negative," Cash said. "Alive but unresponsive. Paramedics are stabilizing him for transport now."

"Have Agent King accompany them."

Understanding dawned. They didn't know where the girls were. Laurel, Kellie Ryles. The others. Without intel from Dillon, they were lost.

No, they weren't. She gripped Cash's arm. "Audra."

"Who?"

"The secretary." Her gaze shot around the room.

Wade sat on the ground nearby. Handcuffed and guarded by two deputies.

"No." She struggled to stand.

Cash helped her to her feet. "What is it?"

"Wade's not the bad guy. He was kidnapped, too." She rushed over. "You've got the wrong guy. Let him go." Grasping Cash's arm, she willed him to understand. "He saved me."

Cash nodded and motioned to the deputies. "Uncuff Mr. DeWitt."

One of them removed the bracelets from Wade's wrists.

"Thank you, Maya," Wade said.

"Are you kidding? After what you and Nina did?" She turned around. "Where is she?"

"They closed her up in the shipping container."

"Until we could determine if she was dangerous," one of the deputies said.

"She's not." Maya turned to Cash. "Nina is the reason we got free. She's an amazing animal. It's not her fault that— Audra! We have to find her."

Cash held up a hand. "Slow down. You're losing me. What about Audra?"

"She's the ringleader."

His brows shot up. "What?"

"Dillon worked for her."

He keyed his radio. "Any sign of an Audra Peterson? Caucasian female, red hair."

"Negative."

"She's here," Maya said. "She left us to meet the buyers. Couldn't have gotten far."

Cash sent the information over the radio. Overstreet gave the command, and the teams geared up for a search.

"What about Laurel?" Maya was sure her sister was in this building as well.

"We've got a team searching the containers," Owen said. "But there are a lot of them. May take a while."

"I can help with that." Wade stepped up to the group. "Nina

was trained as a search and rescue dog. She can find them quicker than we can."

Cash nodded. "Good idea. Owen, escort Mr. DeWitt and his dog to join the search team."

"Copy." Owen and Wade left to get Nina.

The other officers headed out on their assignments. Everyone had something to do. Except her. Once again, she found herself unsure of where she fit.

"What are you going to do?" Maya asked Cash.

"*We* are going to hunt down Miss Peterson."

"We?"

He stepped close, grasping her hands. "If you're up for it." His eyes searched hers.

Part of her wanted to go with Wade. To find Laurel. But there wasn't much she could do there except follow Nina.

The other part wanted to see Audra Peterson captured. The woman behind all this suffering and evil. The woman who had ripped her sister from her family. And from Maya. This was where she could do the most good.

She nodded. "I'm in."

"Good," he said. "Because I made the mistake of leaving you behind once before." He brushed fingers along her cheek. "I won't be making that mistake again."

The intensity in his eyes weakened her knees.

"In this together, right?" she whispered.

Cash pulled her to him, eyes on fire. His lips touched hers, his purpose clear. She met his intensity, pouring all her emotions into the kiss. Being in Cash's arms was like coming home. The place she was supposed to be all along.

Pulling back, he held her face in his hands. His expression tore down all the walls she'd built around her heart. Full, complete acceptance.

With a sigh, he closed his eyes. "As much as I'd love to stay here, we've got a criminal to catch."

"Right." So many emotions swirled through her, but it was time to finish this. Once and for all.

Cash pulled a Glock from his ankle holster and handed it to her. "Stay on my six."

"Copy."

"If I tell you to take cover, you do it."

"Promise."

"One more thing."

"What's that?"

Her breath caught as he smiled, sending her heart galloping again. "I love you, too."

Eyes and ears on full alert, Cash led the way through the warehouse. His radio clicked as other teams cleared their sections. No sign of Audra.

She had to be here. With the building surrounded, she wouldn't have gotten far.

They reached a staircase leading up to a narrow room. Cash stopped at the door and motioned for Maya to get low. They entered the room, which appeared to be a small office.

Empty except for a few pieces of furniture. No hiding places. And no Audra.

Maya nudged him, pointing upward.

In the corner, a small hatch in the ceiling. Must lead to the roof. A desk and filing cabinet beneath would give access to climb through it.

He stepped up to the opening. "Cover me."

She stood behind him, weapon ready. "Always."

Having her with him brought a sense of peace he couldn't explain. Like finding the missing piece of a puzzle. The way he'd felt after giving his life to Christ. Wholeness. Completion.

Cash slipped through the hatch and climbed onto the roof. Chilly night air met him.

A figure moved at the far end.

He pulled his gun. "Stop, Audra."

She turned, cold eyes hostile. "Don't come any closer." A flash of steel in her hand.

Like the night in the old, abandoned warehouse. When he'd found the skeleton. Audra Peterson had taken Elizabeth. He knew it for certain.

Audra paced along the edge of the roof, muttering incoherently. The woman was unraveling, waving her gun around.

He didn't want to shoot her if he could help it. She was the only one who knew where Elizabeth was.

Sound behind him. Maya was on the roof.

"Stay down," he whispered.

It was time for this to stop. Now.

"There's nowhere left to run, Audra," he said. "It's over."

She spun toward him. "I will not go to prison. I'm not like those other women. I won't be like them." She pressed the gun under her chin.

"No, Audra! Please." He'd beg. Plead. Whatever it took. "What about Elizabeth?"

She paused. "What?"

"Elizabeth Fielding," he repeated. "I know you took her. Where is she?"

The hard shell cracked, and Audra's face crinkled in defeat. "She's gone."

Cold settled in his gut, but he pressed on. He had to know. Once and for all.

"What happened?"

"It was a mistake. I… I didn't mean for her to— I gave her too much. Of the insulin. She was my first…acquisition. And… I didn't know. I couldn't wake her up. She was gone."

"Where?" he asked again.

Her head hung. "The DeWitts' kennel. Back side of the property." She raised the gun toward herself again.

Cash aimed.

A board swung, hitting Audra in the head. She went down with a thud.

He stared. Maya had made her way around the roof, unseen, while Audra had been talking. She stood over the woman, board in hand. "Oh no, you don't."

Keeping his weapon trained on Audra, he approached. Stunned but conscious, she lay defeated on the ground.

"Now you can pay for your crimes," Maya said.

He pulled cuffs and fastened them on Audra's wrists. "So much for taking cover," he said to Maya.

She shrugged. "You didn't say where to take cover."

He released a chuckle, thankful this ordeal was ending.

His mic clicked.

"We got them." Owen's voice. "We found the girls."

"Laurel?" Maya's voice cracked.

Cash repeated her question.

"Affirmative," Owen replied.

Her eyes lit up like fireworks.

He nodded toward the roof hatch. "Go. I've got this."

She started to leave but stopped.

"Something wrong?" he asked.

"No. I… I want you with me. When I see her." Tears glistened in her eyes. "I never would have found her without you."

His heart swelled. That she would invite him into this moment meant the world to him.

"Of course." He radioed their location. Watts and Chandler arrived within minutes to take Audra into custody.

Cash and Maya raced through the warehouse.

Cries of relief reached them before the shipping container came into view. They rounded the corner, and Maya pulled up short.

Captives were being led away for medical care. Among them, Cash recognized the woman Dillon had taken from the club. Kellie Ryles. He sent up a prayer of thanks.

Maya's eyes searched the faces, looking for her sister.

"Laurel!" Wade's strangled cry caught their attention.

A young woman with long blonde hair looked up, eyes wide and then full of joy as she raced to her father.

Maya gasped beside Cash, her eyes pooled with tears.

"Go on." He nudged her. "It's time Laurel finally met her sister."

Taking small steps, Maya made her way toward them.

Laurel turned, an elated cry coming from her as she embraced Maya. Wade's arms enveloped them both, and they clung to each other, tears and laughter mingling together.

Emotion thickened his own throat at the loving reunion.

Now, one more reunion to make.

An hour later, he stood on the DeWitts' property. At the edge of the forest, they'd found it. A small mound of dirt.

He called for a shovel and began digging. He was joined by Owen, Addie. Overstreet. And Maya.

He wasn't leaving until he found her.

A sliver of creamy white emerged from the red Georgia clay.

"Elizabeth," he whispered. His eyes misted with tears, blurring his vision.

A hand clapped down on his shoulder. Owen.

"You found her, buddy."

Cash nodded, words trapped in his throat.

A hand slipped into his.

Maya.

Her quiet strength gave him courage to look away. Into her gaze.

The love he saw there filled a void he hadn't even known he had.

"Now we can go home." She glanced down at Elizabeth's remains. "All of us."

EPILOGUE

One year later

Maya crossed the lawn of the DeWitts' estate, cup of punch in one hand and dessert plate in the other. The balancing act, paired with the new, strappy heels she'd purchased yesterday, were a lethal combination.

A hand touched her elbow. "Let me help you with that." Cash grinned. Dressed in a light gray suit, he was a sight to see. But when he turned the full effects of his crystal-blue eyes on her, it was game over.

He took the plate from her and tucked her free hand into the crook of his elbow, guiding her to a table nestled under a massive oak at the edge of the lawn. Once safely seated, she surveyed the festivities.

Laurel's graduation party. A little over a year ago, Maya could only imagine being reunited with her sister. And she'd almost lost that chance because of the actions of a terrible woman.

Thank You, God. She took a deep breath, once again grateful for the chance to reconnect with her sister. After taking a semester off to enter rehab, Laurel had conquered her addiction and come back even stronger. She'd taken extra classes and worked hard to be able to graduate on time.

Audra Peterson and Dillon Cordell, along with their other cohorts, were serving their sentences in prison. The mystery caller who had prompted Cash to visit the warehouse had come forward. A driver from Wade's export business. The man testified that he had been paid to drive the trucks transporting the victims. His conscience had gotten the better of him, so he'd called Cash to tip him off to the location they were being held.

A special joint task force had been formed between the GBI and the FBI to search for the various victims of Audra's trafficking ring. So far, nine women had been rescued and returned to their families. Maya prayed that every one would be found and their families restored. Just like hers had been.

Elizabeth's family had set up a charity to help the victims and asked Cash to serve on the board. The grace they'd extended to him, and being able to help others, had eased some of the pain he carried.

Laurel's laughter carried over the music from the string quartet the DeWitts had hired for the occasion. They'd spared no expense to celebrate their daughter's accomplishments.

Not their *only* daughter, though. Maya glanced down at the silver bracelet on her wrist. The one Helene had given her a month after they'd rescued Laurel from human traffickers. The one that had the word *Daughter* engraved in scroll letters.

The DeWitts had taken her into their family and claimed her as their own. At almost thirty, she was too old to be legally adopted, but Wade and Helene had asked her to consider them her parents. Spending holidays and family outings with them had taken some getting used to, but her new family was conscious of preserving Maya's freedom and independence. They didn't push too much.

It was a new feeling, being part of a family. Of belonging. But one that she was warming to rapidly. She and Laurel met weekly for a sister lunch and talked or texted every day.

"Are you going to eat the rest of that?"

Maya took in her half-eaten slice of cake and then Cash's

hopeful look. Laughter bubbled up and out. "Knock yourself out."

With a grin, he polished off the rest of the cake in two bites. "Thanks!"

Maya wiped a dab of icing from the corner of his mouth. Cash grasped her hand, turning it over to press a kiss to her palm.

His boyish charm was certainly appealing. But the way he made her heart race spoke of the man he was.

Since the events of last year, Cash had been a man of his word. He had shown her what it meant to truly follow Christ, and that love was indeed an action. He protected her heart while at the same time making it very clear his intentions were to capture every part of it.

And he had.

"How about a dance?" Cash held out a hand as the quartet played one of her favorite love songs.

She pointed to her feet in the pretty but impractical shoes. "I'm not sure that's a good idea."

Cash gave her the look that turned her insides to goo. "Please? One dance. I promise I won't let you fall."

But she had. Fallen completely head over heels for Cash Brenner.

She took his hand and let him lead her toward the area designated as the dance floor. They passed Laurel chatting with a couple of friends. Her sister, eyes aglow, reached for a hug.

Maya gave her a quick, tight embrace. Would she ever get used to being able to call her sister whenever she wanted? Or hearing her voice. Seeing her smile. Hugging her so tight.

She hoped not.

On the dance floor, Cash gathered her in his arms, and they swayed to the music. Across the way, Helene caught her gaze and smiled, giving her a quick wink.

Maya's heart was so full. She'd gone from being all alone

to being part of a family. But God had shown her that she had been His all along.

Leaning away, she looked up at Cash.

"What?" he asked.

"Nothing." She smiled. "I'm happy, that's all."

"Good." He glanced away and then back to her. "Maybe, after this song, we can say our goodbyes and head out."

"Got somewhere you need to be?"

He chuckled. "No. Just like to get out of this monkey suit. Maybe take a walk down to the lake with my girl."

She loved the idea of being his.

She remembered the slip of paper tucked between the seats of Cash's Mustang. She'd found it two days ago, while he was pumping gas. A sales receipt for Donahue Jewelers.

Cash was going to propose.

Maybe not tonight. Maybe not tomorrow. But whenever it was, she knew her answer would be yes.

He brushed fingers lightly across her cheek, sending a thrill down to her toes. "I love you, Maya."

"I love you, too."

Tugging his head down, she pressed a kiss to his lips, a promise of many more kisses to come.

Because she wanted nothing more than to belong to Cash Brenner. Forever.

* * * * *

Dear Reader,

I'm so thankful for the opportunity to share this story with you, highlighting the special agents of the Georgia Bureau of Investigation. Any mistakes are my own or embellished for the sake of the story.

Special thanks to Virginia Vaughan and Jessica R. Patch. Your insights were invaluable. And to my agent, Tamela Hancock Murray, and editor, Katie Gowrie, for walking me through every step of this process.

Cash and Maya's journey to happily-ever-after was one that touched my heart deeply. Cash feared loving someone who could leave him. Maya longed for a family but felt she wasn't worthy to be loved. Writing a story where these two broken people could find true love and acceptance was a joy.

We were designed by our Creator to seek the place where we belong. No matter our own family situations, we are all loved and wanted by God. He longs for us to know Him as our Heavenly Father. My prayer is that everyone would have that kind of love.

Let's connect! You can find me on Facebook and Instagram. Sign up for my newsletter at www.hopewelborn.com to stay updated on all my writing news.

Hope